John Creasey –

Born in Surrey, England in 1
there were nine children, Joh
master story teller and international sensation. His more than 600 crime, mystery and thriller titles have now sold 80 million copies in 25 languages. These include many popular series such as *Gideon of Scotland Yard, The Toff, Dr Palfrey* and *The Baron.*

Creasy wrote under many pseudonyms, explaining that booksellers had complained he totally dominated the 'C' section in stores. They included:

Gordon Ashe, M E Cooke, Norman Deane, Robert Caine Frazer, Patrick Gill, Michael Halliday, Charles Hogarth, Brian Hope, Colin Hughes, Kyle Hunt, Abel Mann, Peter Manton, J J Marric, Richard Martin, Rodney Mattheson, Anthony Morton and *Jeremy York.*

Never one to sit still, Creasey had a strong social conscience, and stood for Parliament several times, along with founding the One Party Alliance which promoted the idea of government by a coalition of the best minds from across the political spectrum.

He also founded the British Crime Writers' Association, which to this day celebrates outstanding crime writing. The Mystery Writers of America bestowed upon him the Edgar Award for best novel and then in 1969 the ultimate Grand Master Award. John Creasey's stories are as compelling today as ever.

The Baron Series

Meet the Baron (The Man in the Blue Mask)	1937
The Baron Returns (The Return of Blue Mask)	1937
The Baron Again (Salute Blue Mask)	1938
The Baron at Bay (Blue Mask at Bay)	1938
Alias the Baron (Alias Blue Mask)	1939
The Baron at Large (Challenge Blue Mask!)	1939
Versus the Baron (Blue Mask Strikes Again)	1940
Call for the Baron (Blue Mask Victorious)	1940
The Baron Comes Back	1943
A Case for the Baron	1945
Reward for the Baron	1945
Career for the Baron	1946
The Baron and the Beggar	1947
Blame the Baron	1948
A Rope for the Baron	1948
Books for the Baron	1949
Cry for the Baron	1950
Trap the Baron	1950
Attack the Baron	1951
Shadow the Baron	1951
Warn the Baron	1952
The Baron Goes East	1953
The Baron in France (The Riviera Connection)	1953
Danger for the Baron	1953
The Baron Goes Fast	1954
Nest-Egg for the Baron (Deaf, Dumb and Blonde)	1954
Help from the Baron	1955
Hide the Baron	1956
Frame the Baron (The Double Frame)	1957
Red Eye for the Baron (Blood Red)	1958
Black for the Baron (If Anything Happens to Hester)	1959
Salute for the Baron	1960
A Branch for the Baron (The Baron Branches Out)	1961
Bad for the Baron (The Baron and the Stolen Legacy)	1962
A Sword for the Baron (The Baron and the Mogul Swords)	1963
The Baron on Board	1964
The Baron and the Chinese Puzzle	1964
Sport for the Baron	1966
Affair for the Baron	1967
The Baron and the Missing Old Masters	1968
The Baron and the Unfinished Portrait	1969
Last Laugh for the Baron	1970
The Baron Goes A-Buying	1971
The Baron and the Arrogant Artist	1972
Burgle the Baron	1973
The Baron - King Maker	1975
Love for the Baron	1979

The Baron Goes East

John Creasey

HOUSE OF STRATUS

This edition published in 2014 by House of Stratus, an imprint of
Stratus Books Ltd., Lisandra House, Fore Street,
Looe, Cornwall, PL13 1AD, U.K.
www.houseofstratus.com

Typeset by House of Stratus.

A catalogue record for this book is available from the British Library and the Library of Congress.

ISBN 07551-4336-1
EAN 978-07551-4336-8

CHAPTER ONE

THE BLUE DIAMOND

THE diamond stood on a pad of black velvet, caught in the bright light which shone above the desk. John Mannering sat looking at it dreamily. He was alone in the small office at the rear of his shop – Quinns. Outside, the life of the West End of London throbbed with all its mid-week vigour, but hardly a sound reached Mannering's ears. Inside, within a few paces of the office door, were treasures of the ages. Bejewelled caskets, daggers encrusted with fortunes in precious stones, miniatures painted by masters, pieces of furniture steeped in antiquity. Quinns was a treasure house to which lovers of precious things were drawn from all over the world.

Mannering was oblivious of everything else as he studied the diamond.

It wasn't large. In his strong-room below the shop and approached by a trap-door in the floor, were a dozen larger. It was beautifully cut, but that did not make it exceptional. Yet he had never seen one like it before, and he sat in front of it as if he were worshipping its beauty.

From the centre of the diamond there came light, a blue light. It was as if a tiny blue fire blazed within the stone, yet was cold. This colour spread from the centre to the outer edges, making a cold star of blue fire.

A bell rang, not far off.

Mannering did not move or look away; his face seemed to be carved out of bronze.

There was a tap at the door.

Mannering drew in his breath. Forcing his attention from the diamond to the door seemed to demand a physical as well as mental effort. He called "Come in", but glanced back at the diamond.

A small man with curly grey hair said: "I'm sorry to disturb you, Mr. Mannering."

He stopped, as if silenced by Mannering's expression. Mannering looked as if he were out of this world, living in some fabulous land of the mind. The grey-haired man drew back quickly.

Outside, someone said: "Isn't he there?"

The door closed.

Mannering moved suddenly, pushing the case with the diamond away from him. He had heard the man say "Isn't he there?" and had recognised the voice – that had broken the spell of the blue diamond. He stood up, took out cigarettes and lit one, then opened the door.

The man with the familiar voice spoke again.

"Don't talk out of the back of your neck, Larraby. I'll go in myself."

Mannering stepped into the back of the shop as a man of medium height came towards him, smoking a cigarette. The newcomer was well-dressed in grey, his greying hair was brushed straight back from his forehead, his small moustache was stained yellow with nicotine. He wore a gardenia in his button-hole, and his movements had a nervous briskness.

"Good morning, Bill," welcomed Mannering.

"What's the matter with you?" demanded Superintendent Bristow of New Scotland Yard. "Larraby came out looking as if he'd seen a ghost. What have you got in the office?"

"Nothing that's been stolen!"

"I wonder," said Bristow gruffly.

He was serious enough to make Mannering frown. Larraby, further along the shop, raised his eyebrows, as if to show his despair of all policemen.

"Come and see for yourself," invited Mannering.

Bristow went ahead. There was a small Queen Anne desk with a single chair behind it and room for a winged armchair facing it, with a third in the far corner. This chair was actually on the carpet covering the trap-door which led to the strong-room. The shelves were lined with books. There were a few old prints on the walls, and above the desk a portrait of Mannering. His wife Lorna had painted it.

It was a brilliant work, capturing more than Mannering's good looks: his air of well-being, his natural confidence. It captured something which few people knew was there. A young niece, coming to Quinns for the first time and seeing the portrait, had squeezed Lorna Mannering's hand and cried: "Lorna, darling, no wonder you married him! Why don't you give him a cloak and sword? It would go perfectly with that glint in his eyes and the swagger. John, *darling*, don't you sometimes want to be a pirate? A buccaneer? And go swashbuckling round the world? You're *exactly* right for it."

"Sit down, Bill." Mannering offered cigarettes, went to the door and called: "Tea, Josh, please," and returned to his chair behind the desk. Bristow was staring at the blue diamond. "No bad men about demanding your attention?" inquired Mannering. "No duty calling at police courts and the Old Bailey? No one stealing any jools?"

Bristow took his gaze from the diamond, as if reluctantly. A smile put vitality into his face, taking away the nervous tension. He had good, even features, but somehow missed being handsome.

"Have you lifted any lately?"

"Not for years and years!"

'That's the nearest you've ever got to admitting that you once lived by theft," growled Bristow. As he drew at his cigarette his eyes challenged Mannering's. "What were you up to just now? What made you drive Larraby out?"

"I hardly knew he came in, but heard your dulcet tones and thought I'd better find out what you wanted."

"Try telling the truth."

"You'd never believe me, truth or lie."

"What were you up to? Hiding something? These, for instance." Bristow took an envelope from his pocket, extracted a dozen photographs and handed them across the desk. Mannering studied each, talking as he looked.

"All new to me, Bill. What are they?"

"Photographs of jewels."

"You are in a pleasant mood this morning." He paused. "Whose jewels?"

"The Rangipore Collection," Bristow answered. "Now tell me you've never heard of them. They're the Indian jewels Kallidon brought from New York to offer to old Morency, who is supposed to be interested in anything Indian. They were stolen from him two nights ago. The press gave it far more space than it deserved – but, of course, you never read about jewel robberies, do you?"

There had been headlines in most of the newspapers, for the jewels, worth a small fortune, had been sold in New York by an Indian prince who had clashed with his government.

"If you're asking whether I've been offered them – no," said Mannering.

"What were you hiding when Larraby looked in?"

"Have a look round while you're here."

"I may, at that," said Bristow.

Larraby brought tea in a silver teapot on a silver tray. He then went out, looking at Mannering with eyes which asked: "Trouble?" He was given no answer. Mannering poured out.

Bristow seemed to relax. "Seriously, John, keep your eyes and ears open for the Rangipores. It's not just another jewel robbery."

"It looks like one to me."

"They belonged to this wealthy prince. It's said that a group of zealots in India hate the prince's guts for getting out and living the life of luxury and ease in America on the proceeds of the jewels – which ought to go towards alleviating famine and poverty at home. It's suggested that the zealots meant to get them back and turn them into cash. I don't know if they took them. I do know that it was a good amateur job. Not in your class. They probably won't be offered to Quinns direct, but you or Larraby may hear something."

"Possibly." Mannering was thinking of the zealots – and this blue stone.

"Thanks." Bristow sipped tea, looking at the blue diamond. "Larraby's looking very prosperous. Has he had a rise lately?"

"And promotion," said Mannering. "He's no longer the odd-job man about the place, he's manager. Lorna says I need a holiday. We shall probably go away for a month or so, and Josh will look after things better than most."

Bristow switched his gaze sharply from the diamond.

"I'll never understand you," he said. "Take an ex-convict into Quinns, then give him a golden chance to loot the shop. Don't be surprised if he gets away with everything here."

"Forget it," said Mannering. "You'd trust him as far as I would."

"What's this about a holiday?"

"All inquiries to my wife, it's her idea."

"Abroad?"

"Probably."

"Tell me where,' said Bristow, "and I'll cable the police of the unhappy country that they're going to give hospitality to the cleverest safe-breaker who ever kept out of prison."

Mannering didn't smile; that seemed to surprise Bristow. Mannering offered cigarettes again and poured out another cup of tea. His expression was almost disagreeable.

"There are times when I could dislike you," he said. "When are you going to stop making dark allusions to my imaginary past? You're getting worse. We can't meet in the street without you making a crack, and if someone else is with us it's a cryptic comment that sets them wondering. I'm getting tired of it."

Bristow listened and watched with rounded eyes.

"You think I was once the jewel-thief known as the Baron," said Mannering in the same even voice. "You've never been able to prove it, and you never will. During the past ten years I've risked my neck a dozen times, and my freedom a dozen more, to help you put a criminal in dock and in jail. Let's have a few more references to that and fewer allusions to the Baron."

"My, my," said Bristow. "What's happened to your sense of humour?"

"You need a joke for a sense of humour."

"Hm." Bristow's eyes were still questioning. "How old are you? Nearing middle-age? Lord save you from becoming as pompous as you sound now." He finished his tea and stood up. "You'll keep an eye open for this Indian stuff, won't you?" He touched the photographs.

"I've already said I will."

"Thanks." Bristow turned towards the door, then looked back. His gaze fell on the blue diamond again. "What's the blue stone?"

"A diamond," said Mannering heavily. He leaned across the desk, picked up the case and handed it to Bristow. Outside the trade, few people knew so much as he about precious stones.

Bristow studied and admired.

"Perfect. I can't say that I've heard about blue diamonds."

"I hadn't either, until this turned up. It's Indian. Old Aly Phiroshah sent it and said that he would write and tell me what it was all about. I haven't heard from him yet." The gleam made a brief return to Mannering's eyes as suspicion leapt into Bristow's. "Legal cargo, by air – on the manifest and checked by Customs."

"Who suggested it wasn't?" Bristow hedged. "Isn't Phiroshah dead yet? When he was in London ten years ago he looked as if he were dying on his feet."

"He's still alive," Mannering said and took the diamond back. "India's very busy in the jewel trade."

"It's an odd coincidence," Bristow said, and didn't add: "If it is a coincidence." "Do you think Phiroshah is honest?"

"As the day."

Mannering saw Bristow to the door and watched him go along Hart Row, the narrow turning off Bond Street where Quinns and a few other small, narrow-fronted shops were situated. Quinns was the narrowest and probably the most exclusive; most of the atmosphere of Hart Row came from it. It was Elizabethan, with nothing built on. The roof was of red tiles, to which lichen gave a softening green. There were gables and old oak, and on the fascia board the single word Quinns painted in gilt in Old English lettering.

The window held a single jewelled dagger. This rested on black velvet, and the jewels in the hilt seemed to give life and light to the blackness. Mannering saw this out of the corner of his eye as he turned and walked back along the narrow shop. On either side of the passage antiques stood in gloom, but lights could be switched on to show each piece to advantage. Prints, miniatures, Dutch panels and some framed Chinese embroideries were on the walls. Mannering walked past all these and turned into the office.

Larraby stood contemplating the blue diamond; his love for precious stones was like a man's love for a woman. He turned his gentle face to Mannering, but didn't speak. They smiled with complete understanding. Then the bell of the shop door rang.

"I'll see who it is." Larraby turned, then stopped in the passage, narrow just outside the door. "Mr. Mannering," he said softly, "I think Phiroshah's messenger has arrived."

Mannering picked up the jewel-case, snapped it shut, and slipped it into his pocket before following Larraby.

At the far end of the shop stood a young woman dressed in a dark red sari; it was as if she had been transported from India and dropped into Quinns. She made no move as Mannering passed Larraby and approached her.

CHAPTER TWO

THE MESSENGER

As Mannering smiled at the girl, Larraby switched on a lamp concealed in the ceiling and giving just sufficient light to show the visitor more clearly, without being harsh. But no light could be harsh enough to harm her. She was young. Her complexion was perfect, and she was beautiful; that was the only word, none other was needed. She had large dark-brown eyes, raven-black hair drawn straight back from her forehead with a centre parting. She wore nothing over the sari, which swept almost to her small feet, which were criss-crossed by the straps of open sandals. On her forehead was a single scarlet spot, her caste mark.

"Good morning," Mannering said.

"Good morning." Her voice was soft and her English good, almost without accent; that didn't surprise him. "Are you Mr. John Mannering?"

"Yes."

"I have a message for you from Aly Phiroshah."

"I've been expecting it."

"You have the diamond?"

"Yes." It was easy to smile at her. "Come with me." He led her to the office. Larraby wasn't in sight, but was undoubtedly watching.

The girl did not look about the office, but her gaze went straight to the blue diamond as Mannering took it out again. She sat down, murmuring "Thank you" and still looking at the stone. In the brighter light here, no flaw showed in her beauty.

In the same way as Bristow, Mannering and Larraby, she had to force herself to look away from the diamond. She took a small handbag from beneath the folds of her sari. Her fingernails were painted the same colour as the spot on her forehead.

She took out a letter, which was sealed with a red wax and with some Hindi lettering. Mannering recognised it as Phiroshah's seal. It was familiar to dealers in precious stones and to collectors all over the world.

"Thank you." Mannering took and opened it. He wasn't completely at his ease, partly because of the girl's gaze, which had a candour that seemed very youthful yet – sad? It might be partly due to the fact that precious stones from India were in the news.

He wasn't surprised to find the letter written by hand. Phiroshah's writing was copper-plate and his English good if a little precise.

"Dear John Mannering,

The bearer of this letter is my daughter, Shani. She will tell you everything that I would like to tell you myself. I ask only that you pay as much attention to her as you would to me and, if you can respond favourably to her request, that you lose little time.

"With felicitations, my friend,

"Aly Phiroshah."

Shani watched Mannering gravely as he read, and was intent as he looked up. He tried to see some likeness to her father in her. The old man was in his eighties. He had seemed ancient ten years ago, when Mannering had met him. Mannering recalled a wizened face, bony, gaunt; a Ghandi of a man, bald-headed, with wrinkled flesh at his eyes, much more beneath his chin. Shani waited for Mannering to speak. "Why did he send you and not one of his sons?" Mannering asked.

Phiroshah had been proud of his sons.

Shani raised her hands a little, drawing attention to their olive colour, their smallness and exquisite shape.

"They are dead," she announced.

"*All* of them?" Shocked surprise sharpened his voice. He had known of at least two sons, and had believed that the old Hindu had several others by his three wives.

"Those who matter," Shani said.

She did not elaborate; he was sure that she wouldn't, as sure that if he asked a question she would answer truthfully. Her father had commanded it, and her father's word was law. The difficulty was to overcome surprise, choose the questions wisely, to find out all he could. Phiroshah had sent her with a message about the blue diamond, not about his personal affairs.

He could ask her what she meant by "those who matter", but would it really help him? He pulled the case towards him and picked it up; it seemed a sacrilege to hold the diamond between his fingers. He began to speak, when the telephone bell rang – a short ring, meaning that Larraby wanted to speak to him. He put down the case, frowning; he frowned too easily these days. He lifted the receiver, said "Hallo", and remembered constraint had fallen between him and Bristow, because he was touchy and scowled too much.

"What is it?" His voice was gruff.

"Mrs. Mannering has just arrived," Larraby said. "She is paying off her taxi."

"Oh. All right, thanks." Mannering rang off. He wished Lorna hadn't chosen this moment to come. "I'm sorry, Miss Phiroshah, but my wife has just arrived. I won't keep you a minute." He stepped towards the door, leaving the diamond on the desk. There was only one way out of the office – by the door. There were ventilators and air-conditioning, but no windows. In any case, wasn't she Phiroshah's daughter?

Lorna was halfway along the shop, smiling at Larraby.

Lorna, smiling, was something to see. Her dark-grey eyes sparkled, her teeth showed, she looked young. She *was* young. There was only two years' difference in their ages and Mannering was nearing forty – but there were times when she seemed ten years younger. She had seen him and glanced his way, but still spoke to

Larraby.

"Yes, Josh, I agree with you. We'll see what we can do." Larraby stood aside, and Lorna approached. She moved gracefully. She was stylishly dressed in a tailored suit and a wide mink collar. Her small hat concealed only a little of her glossy, wavy hair – hair as dark as Shani's. "Hallo, darling." She said "darling" as if she meant it. "Am I butting in? Josh says that Phiro's messenger has turned up."

"You're just in time to hear the story." He pressed her hand. "Congratulations."

She laughed. "On what?"

"I don't know, but you couldn't look as happy as you do if you hadn't good news."

"Oh, nothing," she said and laughed again. "I've just sold a picture to a collector from Paris. Ridiculous, isn't it?" She stripped off her gloves. "Coals to Newcastle."

"Hideous simile." Mannering shuddered. He was delighted, and knew that she was. His spirits rose. "Tell me about it after we've heard what Shani has to say."

"Shani?"

"The old chap's daughter."

"Daughter?"

"He may be an old Hindu and a stickler for convention, but he's moved with the times and believes in the emancipation of women," said Mannering. "He's much more like a Parsee than a Hindu in some ways." He pressed her hand. "We'll celebrate tonight." He opened the office door and ushered Lorna in.

Shani stood up.

Mannering watched the two women; Lorna completely at ease, Shani – embarrassed? It was hard to say. She was still grave. They sat down, Lorna in an old William and Mary slung chair in the far corner. Mannering picked up the diamond and seemed to forget Lorna. She would expect that.

"Why did he send this by one plane and you by another?" asked Mannering. "You must have left Bombay almost at the same time. This didn't arrive until this morning."

"That was what he intended – that the diamond should arrive first and I should follow it." Shani didn't smile. "He did not wish me to carry it."

"Why not?"

"He is frightened of it."

Lack of emphasis made the words very effective. Lorna watched Shani, and Mannering could imagine how she would react to the word frightened. Soon she would be saying: "John, keep out of this." He tried to be casual.

"Of course, it's a valuable jewel to travel with; it's always safer to rely on the usual channels." Bristow had hoped that he wasn't going to become pompous. He sounded too pompous now, and it irritated him. He was falling short in concentration. Of late he'd been uncertain in temper, unpredictable in mood – as Bristow knew.

"It wasn't that," Shani said. "It is thought that there will be another attempt to steal the diamond."

Lorna was as grave as the Indian girl, and as intent. She must know about the zealots and their "war" against a prince, and the theft of Indian jewels here in London.

"Another?" he asked.

"It has happened twice. Two of my brothers died defending it."

Again she spoke without emphasis, but the words had the force of a bullet. Mannering sensed danger, as if it were an aura surrounding the girl. He fought to keep his tone and manner matter-of-fact.

"When?" he asked.

"Yusuf died two months ago," said Shani. "Ali only two weeks ago. It was then that my father decided to write to you. He attempted to explain what had happened and what he hoped you would do by letter." She raised her hands slightly and made the crimson folds of the sari move, like rippling red water. "It was so difficult, so he decided to send me to explain, and the diamond to show you that he was in earnest."

Phiroshah knew his love of precious stones, knew how the blue diamond would affect him, so he had sent the diamond first, making sure of his interest.

Mannering didn't look at Lorna.

"How did your father get the stone?" he asked Shani.

"You will understand much," she said slowly. "Since the self-government of India and the weakening of the power and the authority of the princes, many of them are selling jewels. It is not dishonest. The Government does not object. Sometimes the princes must sell in order to find the money for taxes or to put in hand the works which the Government demands. Sometimes they sell and live abroad. So my father has been very busy. For fifty years, now, he has sold more precious stones to the princes than any other man in India. Many have bought from him rather than from agents and dealers in England and America and elsewhere. All that you know." Her story wasn't simply a recitation of simple facts; there was feeling in her voice. She disapproved of what was happening in India, as her father disapproved; Phiroshah had never been a politician, but had loved the old order and the old ways – perhaps partly because he had become a millionaire through them.

"Yes," said Mannering.

"Four months ago the Maharajah of Ganpore visited my father secretly. That had happened before. The Maharajah has never boasted of his riches, never flaunted them. He prefers to buy and to sell quietly. He brought this blue diamond and other jewels. The others he sold. He told my father that he had a collection of the blue diamonds known to few. He wanted to find out what each stone was worth. He left the blue diamond with my father, and—my father sent Yusuf, his younger and well-trusted son, to America with it. In many ways, he would have liked to offer these diamonds to an English buyer, but—" She shrugged her shoulders in a gesture that was almost European. "In New York, the market is so much better, and so many more can afford to buy."

"Yes," said Mannering.

"Yusuf flew to New York, saw several of the big dealers, and met some principals who might be interested in buying. The negotiations were prolonged. He flew back to Bombay for further instructions from my father, and all the time he kept the jewel with him. There was an understanding with the Maharajah that only my father or one of the family should have charge of it. Then Yusuf flew back to

New York. Within two days he had been murdered.

"He had known of the danger, for he sent the diamond back through a trusted agent, the day before he died. The news of his death made my father ill. Ali, my older brother, was in charge in Bombay. He received the stone. He was unhappy about what had happened and reluctant to go further. He took it himself to the Maharajah, to say that now that my father was ill and Yusuf dead it was impossible to continue with the negotiations. He reached the Maharajah with the diamond, but not before he was severely injured. He went by train; the train was held up by dacoits. He was searched and tortured, but saved the diamond. He died within an hour of returning it to the Maharajah." She looked away from Mannering for the first time and glanced at the stone, and there was bitterness in her voice. "You understand now why my father is frightened."

Into the hush which followed Mannering said: "Yes, but I can't understand why he is still handling the diamond. Are you going to tell me that?"

CHAPTER THREE

THE REQUEST

As he spoke, Mannering glanced at Lorna. Over the years she had suffered torment because he had sacrificed so much to his love of jewels. She had shared all the risks in the days when he had been the Baron, jewel-thief extraordinary; through the days of the metamorphosis which had turned him into a collector of precious stones and a hunter of thieves; and as he was today. But she had never wholly shared the rewards. She lacked his passion, almost his mania, for jewels. She would hate this.

She was smiling.

Shani said quietly: "I am surprised that you should ask why my father is still handling the diamond, Mr. Mannering. I believe that you know him. My brother made the decision to return it to the Maharajah while my father was sick. On his recovery, my father went in person to the Palace of Ganpore and promised that he would find the best price he could for the blue diamonds. He asks me to tell you, Mr. Mannering, that he had considered approaching you from the beginning, and sent Yusuf to America only because he believed that more money could be obtained there. He had good reason for wanting to secure the highest price for the Maharajah."

"I'm sure he has," said Mannering.

"Now that murder has twice been committed, and it had become obvious that the murderers wanted the blue diamond, my father needs more than a dealer in precious stones. He remembered how you had helped him when he was in London and some of his jewels were stolen. He also recalled that Scotland Yard appeared to have the highest regard for you. At the request of the Maharajah of Ganpore, he did not inform the police in Bombay, Calcutta or New York. Instead, he decided to send me to plead with you."

Lorna moved a little in her chair.

"His request is simple," said Shani. "That you should come to India soon. Visit the Maharajah, find out all you can of the blue diamonds, and find out who committed murder to try to get this one. He is insistent, please understand, that he is not asking that you undertake the avenging of his sons; only that you find out who is behind this violence. He will make sure that you are well rewarded."

Mannering said mildly: "I'm sure he would."

"He says also that you might think it best to start in New York, but he asks that you come first to India. There is reason to believe that the murderer was one of our people, in New York; and, of course, dacoits were employed in the murder of Ali."

Dacoits? Zealots?

Shani finished, but did not shift her position, simply stared with a grave intentness more insistent than a spoken plea.

"I know nothing about conditions in India," Mannering said. "If it happened in London, even New York, I might be your man. But in Bombay or Ganpore—"

"My father believes that you could help because he knows that he can trust you," Shani said simply. "He knows of no one else so trustworthy and with such experience. I hope that I have made that clear."

Lorna said gently: "Very clear. How long may we have to decide?"

Shani hesitated, as if surprised by the "we". She looked from Mannering to Lorna and back.

"I am to cable him with the answer. Also, I am to return as quickly as I can. I have a reservation on an aircraft leaving London Airport on Friday."

This was Wednesday.

"Where are you staying?"

"At the Mirabar Hotel, Kensington."

"Darling, why don't you promise to telephone Miss Phiroshah

there this afternoon Say at three o'clock. You'll have time to think about it, and we'll have time to talk." Lorna seemed eager. Mannering still didn't understand why her mood was still buoyant.

"I'd rather make it seven o'clock," Mannering said. "Will that suit?"

"Thank you, it will be very good of you." Shani started to get up.

"Wait a minute," Mannering said. "I'll get you a taxi."

Shani sank back in her chair, and Lorna started to speak as the door closed on him. Mannering felt as he might on a clear, crisp autumn day – invigorated. Lorna had helped, but the blue diamond had started all this; the girl's story had given it urgency, and the theft of the Rangipore jewels had rounded it off. Here was certainly work for the Baron.

Larraby was polishing a gold necklace which had once adorned the neck of an Elizabethan beauty.

"Josh," said Mannering, "have you looked outside lately?"

"Only when the Indian lady and Mrs. Mannering—"

"Look now," said Mannering, "for a taxi standing in the street, or an Indian watching the shop. Change the position of that dagger in the window and then pop outside and admire it."

Larraby said softly: "It's like *that*, is it?"

"It could be."

"I won't be long." Larraby turned towards the window, and Mannering to a recess at the back of the shop, which led to twisting oak stairs and the storerooms above. A telephone, an extension to the main instrument in the office, stood on a ledge in the recess. He dialled a Temple Bar number.

"Good morning, this is Plummer's Detective Agency."

"Is Mr. Plummer in? This is John Mannering."

"*Good* morning. I think he will be to you, Mr. Mannering!" The girl went off the line, and Mannering waited, watching Larraby through a small window in the wall of the recess. Larraby was standing on the pavement and apparently giving all his attention to the jewelled dagger.

A man said: "Hallo, Mr. Mannering."

"Jeff, can you do something for me, yourself, at once?"

"Gladly do," said Jeff Plummer.

"Come round at once, by car. I've been talking to an Indian girl, and she'll be leaving in the next ten minutes. I want you to follow her."

"Only traffic will delay me," said Plummer.

"Fly over it!" Mannering rang off and moved out of the recess as Larraby came back; excitement gleamed in his eyes.

"Well, Josh?"

"She was followed," declared Larraby. 'There is an Indian lounging at the corner – a dark-skinned young man. And there is a taxi just along the road, with the driver in it and his flag down. He might be waiting for someone at one of the other shops."

"And he might not," said Mannering softly. "Josh, go and get a cab. Be back in a quarter of an hour. Lock the door when you go out, and ring the bell three times when you come back. All clear?"

"It is indeed," said Larraby. "Is this about the blue diamond?"

"Yes. Are you surprised?"

"Nothing would surprise me about that jewel," Larraby said. He went out, letting down the catch at the shop door and slamming it. Mannering walked to the front of the shop and stood at one side of the window. He saw the dark-skinned man at a nearby corner, wearing a dark-blue suit. He was handsome, with wavy black hair, heavy with oil. He was looking at a newspaper.

The taxi was in the other direction.

Mannering went back to the office. Lorna was asking about living conditions in India. Shani answered politely, then turned to Mannering.

"Is my taxi here, please?"

"My man is having difficulty," Mannering said. "They're not easy at midday. He'll soon find one." He sat on a corner of the desk. "You may not believe it, but I'm not really careless with that stone. I had to collect it from the Customs this morning. You timed your visit well, didn't you?"

Shani smiled. "I was told that you had been to the Customs office, and so I guessed."

"Who told you?"

"My father did not send me alone."

Mannering pictured a young man standing at the corner and reading a newspaper.

"I should think not!"

Shani stood up slowly, and for the first time she really pleaded. "You remember my father. He is a good man, and he is old – very old. The shock of the deaths of his two sons was very great. We who love him were afraid he would die. But he lived. Now, I know, he lives only that we find out the truth. He has much faith in you. Please do not disappoint him."

When Larraby returned, the taxi was still waiting, the Indian was still at his corner. Plummer, a plump, fair-haired and fresh-faced forty, had turned into Hart Row and gone into a shop doorway further along.

Mannering locked the diamond in a wall-safe before he and Lorna saw Shani to the door and into Larraby's taxi. They waited until the driver started his engine, then hurried through the shop and up the stairs. The window of a showroom filled with oil paintings overlooked Hart Row. The Mannerings stood close to the window.

The waiting taxi started off immediately after the girl's; the Indian on the corner jumped into it. Plummer appeared and followed only a few yards behind at the wheel of an open two-seater.

He disappeared.

Lorna said: "You laid that all on quickly, darling."

"Trifles," said Mannering. He took her hands, squeezed. "I'm slipping. It took me ten minutes to realise what has got into you. You think India would be a good place for a holiday, do you?"

"Darling," said Lorna, "haven't you always wanted to see the Taj Mahal? By moonlight? And haven't you always wanted—"

"No."

"And think of the different subjects I can paint."

"Such as the Taj Mahal by night and day. So now I've a pair of you to deal with."

"Oh, that's easy," said Lorna. "Just say yes to Shani and yes to me. I'm sorry that we'll have to fly; I'd much rather go by sea, but it takes three weeks. Darling, it's the first time I've really been able to enthuse over something reckless. Don't say you've any doubts."

Mannering laughed. "Not serious doubts." But she hadn't really explained her mood. He turned towards the door. I'm going to telephone Phiroshah. We'll talk to him before we talk to the girl again. There's an outside chance that she isn't his daughter."

"I suppose you're wise, but there isn't much doubt, is there?"

At the head of the stairs Mannering squeezed her arm.

"If we do take on this job we've one particular thing to get into our minds. Different values, different standards, different methods. You can't judge an Indian by the same standards as you can a European. It's not a case of better or worse – it's simply different. With luck we'll find out what all this is about and you'll have some time for sightseeing and your brushes but—"

Lorna said: "You're really dubious about it, aren't you?"

Her tone echoed her surprise. Hadn't she connected this with newspaper stories of Indian fanatics and the London robbery?

He tightened his grip on her arm, and his voice was suddenly loud.

"Of course I am. I don't think I'll go to India for Shani or for anyone else." He released her and went downstairs quickly but softly, leaving her standing at the top – no longer puzzled, but alarmed. He reached the door at the foot of the stairs.

A dark-skinned man stood at the office door. Another was bending over Larraby, who lay face downwards on the floor of the shop.

CHAPTER FOUR

PRESENT FOR BRISTOW

MANNERING heard a faint rustle behind him; Lorna was creeping down the stairs. From the moment he had been warned by a gasping sound less than twenty seconds had passed. The one dark-skinned man was still bending over Larraby, the other remained by the door. Both would move within the next few seconds. Both had heard the Mannerings talking, and would notice the silence after Mannering's loud remark meant for their ears.

Lorna was close behind Mannering.

"Back," he whispered. "Noisily. Shout out to me."

She turned at once. He withdrew his head as the man by Larraby began to turn. She called in a slightly husky voice: "John – are you in there?"

He didn't try to answer, but pressed close against the wall at the foot of the stairs. The men would probably come to investigate together, and would be armed. He took out his cigarette-case, then stretched up for a match lock pistol hanging on the wall above the doorway. He could just reach it.

"Oh, there you are!" Lorna's voice came clearly; she never needed much telling about tactics. The two men should be reassured.

A head of oily, wavy, dark hair.

Yusuf and Ali had been murdered . . .

Mannering smashed the butt of the match lock on the head, moved forward and thrust his victim backwards. The other was a yard behind him; both had knives. The first man fell against his companion. Mannering went forward swiftly and smashed at the hand holding the knife. The knife dropped. The second man twisted himself free and ran towards the door, leaping over Larraby.

Mannering stood to one side. The man might have a gun as well as a knife. There was no shooting. The door opened and closed with a bang and the fugitive raced along the street towards Bond Street.

The other was trying to sit up. He had one hand at his head, and his eyes were dazed. Mannering hauled him to his feet by his coat lapels and pushed him into an old winged armchair. He struck him sharply on the side of the chin, pulled his arms behind the chair and tied the wrists together with picture cord.

No one approached from the street; so the fugitive, even if noticed, hadn't been seen to run from Quinns.

Footsteps clattered on the stairs – Lorna in a hurry. She burst into sight.

"John—"

"All over," said Mannering. "Call Bristow for me, will you?" He hurried to Larraby, who was groaning – a good sign. He straightened him out carefully, felt his head, discovered a good-sized bump but nothing broken. He lifted his manager into another armchair, took off his own coat and wrapped it round Larraby, and then stood back. Larraby's eyelids were flickering.

"All safe," Mannering said. "Take it easy, Josh." Loma, talking into the telephone, glanced round.

"Bristow's not there. He's never there when we want him."

"Do they know when he'll be back?"

"Any minute."

"We'll ring later." Mannering went back to Larraby, who was licking his lips. Lorna went into the kitchenette behind the shop. She would put on a kettle and make some tea, and probably bring a blanket – one Larraby used when he occasionally stayed up all night on some special job. "We caught one of them. Josh; it's all right."

"I—I'm sorry, Mr. Mannering. They were *inside*. Must have been here for hours. In that cupboard." He pointed to a big Elizabethan cupboard which filled one corner. "See, the door's open."

Mannering inspected the cupboard, and saw footmarks on the

inside. The men could easily have slipped into the shop during the morning. There had been a delivery of pictures, men had been coming in and out, and he had been in the office while Larraby had superintended. The two chief assistants were off – one sick, one on holiday.

Mannering went back to the Indian as Lorna came out, with a cup of tea in her hand, and a blanket over her arm. She pulled away Mannering's coat and tucked the blanket round Larraby. He was all right, he could get up. She made him sit there and sip hot, sweet tea.

The Indian was stirring.

Mannering checked the cord at his wrists, then went to the street door, slipping on his coat. Two or three people were outside, two of them looking at a milliner's next door; a shop where a piece of tulle and some straw were turned into a fortune. A big policeman was coming from the corner, ponderous and familiar. Mannering beckoned, and he hurried.

"Yes, sir?"

"We've had a little trouble," said Mannering. "My wife's here with Larraby, who's been hurt. I've to take a prisoner to the Yard right away, for Mr. Bristow. Keep an eye on things while I'm gone, will you?"

"What kind of trouble, Mr. Mannering?"

"Shoplifting." That would serve.

Mannering went back along the street to a small car-park, free to anyone but used mainly by the tenants of Hart Row. His black Rolls Bentley stood in the corner. He drove to the shop. The policeman was at the open door, a strong sense of duty keeping him there instead of inside asking the obvious questions. Mannering said enough to convince him that he was expected at the Yard and went to the back of the shop.

Lorna left Larraby, who looked better.

The Indian had come round.

"What are you going to do?" Lorna asked.

"Make him a present for Bristow," said Mannering. He didn't speak to the man as he untied the cord, pulled him out of the chair, then bound his wrists behind him more tightly. Lorna looked dubious.

"Wouldn't it be better to question him yourself?"

"He won't talk, except under pressure, and with a copper on the doorstep I daren't press. If I behave nice and correctly, Bristow will probably tell the Bombay police that I'm worth looking after. It would be nice to have friends at court in Bombay."

"So you've decided."

"I couldn't disappoint you when you'd set your mind on it!" Mannering gripped the Indian's shoulder and pushed him towards the door. Lorna sat down on a stool, near Larraby, watching her husband. Mannering moved quickly and easily. He knew exactly what he was doing; probably he was working out moves that lay weeks ahead. She marvelled at it, at everything about him.

Larraby said: "It's amazing, isn't it? He's been touchy and difficult for weeks. Now this comes along, and he's himself in two shakes of a lamb's tail. I'm all right now, Mrs. Mannering, I'll get up."

She could not stop him.

Mannering bundled the Indian into the back of the car while the policeman held the door, then took the wheel. He drove off, thinking as much of Lorna as of the man in the back. She had been urging him to go away for a few months, leaving Larraby in charge; perhaps she saw this as the great chance.

Forget that.

He could take his prisoner to a quiet spot and try questioning him, but he had little time and it would be risky. The policeman had probably called the Yard or his station by now. Mannering headed for the Yard.

What should he tell Bristow? Any part of the story about the blue diamond? Or anything that would connect the prisoner with that and old Phiroshah?

Mannering reached the big new building of Scotland Yard which housed the Criminal Investigation Department. The man on duty at the gates recognised, saluted and waved him inside. A dozen cars were parked at the foot of an imposing flight of stone steps. Mannering helped his prisoner out, watched by the gate duty man and two others who stood at the top of the steps.

The sergeant at the top of the steps saluted.

"Brought us a present, Mr. Mannering?"

"That's right. Think Mr. Bristow will like him?"

"Shouldn't be surprised. Does he know you're coming?"

"I think so. I was told he'd be in."

"Came back ten minutes ago," said the sergeant. "I'll telephone him. Want any help??"

"No, thanks, but if you—"

Mannering broke off, felt the Indian writhe and twist, actually saw the cord fall from his wrists. The man swung on his toes and dived between Mannering and the sergeant towards the steps. He was as swift as an arrow. Mannering shot out a leg and the man kicked against it and fell. The sergeant, a portly fifty, went down in a flying tackle, caught the man's legs and hugged them.

Mannering said mildly: "Perhaps I'd better have some help after all."

"Slippery devil." The sergeant slid a pair of handcuffs from his pocket, snapped them on and stood up, yanking the man after him. "Smith, go along with Mr. Mannering. He won't slip those in a hurry, sir."

"I'm sure he won't." Mannering held the Indian's right arm, the policeman his left, and they walked to the lift and went up to Bristow's office.

Mannering tapped on Bristow's door and received a gruff "Come in". He opened the door and pushed the Indian inside. Bristow gaped. "Thanks, Smith," Mannering said to the constable, then pushed the prisoner into one of two armchairs in Bristow's long, narrow office. This overlooked the Thames Embankment, and May's sunshine had brought the leaves of the plane trees to pale green beauty; one was just outside the window, its nearer branches almost within arm's reach.

"There you are," said Mannering. "Good for the evil aspersions you were so busy with this morning." He grinned. "How's that for pomposity?"

The Indian sat silent and sullen, meeting Bristow's gaze defiantly.

Bristow lit a cigarette, studied first the Indian, then Mannering, and made a palpable effort to regain his self-control. He blew smoke-rings as he said: "Isn't there a police station near you?"

"I could have tried Great Marlborough Street, but as I wanted a word with you I thought I'd bring him in person. Care to have him charged with assault on Carraby while we have a chat?"

Bristow said: "I wonder what you really want." But he sent for a sergeant and gave instructions. The sullen Indian was taken out. Bristow lit a cigarette from the stub of one that was only half-smoked, leaned back in his chair, and said: "Now what?"

Mannering murmured: "In confidence, off the record, not for publication."

"I'm not a newspaperman."

"Of course," went on Mannering, "I could just leave things as they are and you guessing. But I thought you'd like to know what he really came for."

Bristow smoothed down his moustache.

"That blue diamond. Where's the mystery?"

He was no fool. He could be obstinate, could refuse to listen to a story in confidence. If he refused, Mannering need say nothing but would not gain what he wanted – recommendation to the Bombay police. He sat back, smiling.

"All right, let's have it," Bristow said.

He did not have to help, even when he knew the story. Mannering had been the Baron, and no policeman could forget that. Any policeman, even Bristow, who had become a friend, might rebel against recommending him to another police force, especially in a country bristling with jewels.

Mannering felt on edge, briskly though he talked.

CHAPTER FIVE

TICKETS FOR TWO

BRISTOW listened, Mannering talked and thought. There were a dozen reasons why the Yard man should decide that this was an official matter, and that the only help he could give was official. Mannering "forgot" to say that Yusuf Phiroshah had been murdered in New York; "forgot" to mention that the Maharajah of Ganpore was believed to have a store of the blue diamonds. Old Aly Phiroshah wanted help; it would be a business trip and holiday combined. If he, Mannering, ran into trouble, it would be invaluable if he could call on the Indian police knowing that he had the moral support of Bristow of the Yard.

He etched in the raid by the two Indians; obviously they had believed that Shani had the diamond and had broken in to try to get it. The smaller of the two men had escaped, the larger was the prisoner.

"What's his name?" Bristow asked.

"I don't know."

"So you really want to convince me that you haven't questioned him."

"It can't be half an hour since I caught him," Mannering pointed out.

"Almost a reformed character, aren't you? Well, whatever happens won't be on my doorstep. I'll tell them at Bombay, Delhi and Calcutta what a wonderful amateur detective you are and how often you've helped the Yard. I'll forget to tell them that you're the best man at cracking a crib in England."

Mannering kept a straight face.

"That's fine, Bill."

"Lorna going?" asked Bristow.

"She'd like to."

"I don't know that I'd take her," said Bristow thoughtfully. "I'm not sure that India's a place for a white woman these days."

"Don't tell me *you* know India."

Bristow grinned. "Bombay, Calcutta and Madras—yes. Years ago." He picked up the telephone and said into it: "Get me Chamberlin." He held on, and added for Mannering's benefit: "Chamberlin knows more about India than anyone here. He went to study drugs there, a year ago. It strengthens our hand when we're dealing with our floating Indian population. We get some bad ones. Hallo—Chamberlin. Bristow . . . Do you know if old Kana is still working at Bombay? . . . He is? . . . Good, thanks." Bristow rang off and chuckled. "Kana's one of the Chiefs of Police. He was high up, even when the upper crust of their C.I.D. was European. He's a shrewd chap, and I think he'll tolerate you. Give him my personal regards, and take him a couple of pounds of barley sugar pieces. Don't let him get near Lorna; she'll scream out that she wants to paint him, and that would mean leaving her alone with him for too long."

"Kana," echoed Mannering. "Bill, after this I forgive you for everything."

"Anyone who's going to try to tackle a job in India has my sympathy. We shall probably have to send wreaths! Now what about this chap you brought in?"

"You could look for his friend and others who might work with him," said Mannering. "They could have followed Shani here, or they may be local people who've had instructions from India."

"And I'm to keep you informed," said Bristow dryly. "When are you going?"

"As soon as we can get on a plane."

"I'm told they're pretty full," said Bristow. "No doubt you can pull enough strings to go when you want to." He stood up. Don't take too many chances, John. I shouldn't think Phiroshah or his Maharajah friend are worth dying for.'

Bristow might know more than he'd said.

Mannering went straight back to Quinns. The policeman was still outside; inside, Lorna was trying to cope with a customer, and there was no sign of Larraby. In the middle of earnest discussions on the merits of a piece of sixteenth-century Arab silver, Plummer came in. The customer bought the silver and went off practically cooing with delight. Plummer smoothed down his fair hair.

"So that's how you make money."

"That's one way," said Mannering.

"I'll change jobs any time you like." Plummer smoothed down his hair again, a mannerism nothing could change.

"Where's Josh?" Mannering asked Lorna.

"He wouldn't stay after Mr. Plummer called to say he had followed Phiroshah's daughter to the Mirabar in Kensington, and wanted someone to watch there."

"That's right," said Plummer. "Josh was anxious to prove he wasn't hurt. The man in the taxi went as far as the Mirabar and then moved on. He's staying at a boarding house in Bloomsbury. Name of Banu. He arrived in London two days ago by air, and he's officially on business. I don't know what business. Larraby's watching the Mirabar hotel, but he's anxious to get back here. I've sent for a man to relieve him. All you want is to have the girl looked after, I take it."

"Give me the address of Banu's boarding-house, will you?" Mannering asked.

Plummer scribbled on a piece of paper.

Mannering tucked the note away. "Thanks for everything, Jeff."

"A pleasure." Plummer's hand strayed to his hair again. "Be careful with these people. If you get a bad one, he'll be deadly."

"Tell that to my wife," said Mannering.

Lorna laughed it off, but was thoughtful when Plummer had gone. Mannering dropped the catch at the door, and they went into the office. He took the blue diamond out of the wall safe and laid it on his desk; the light gave it fiery blue beauty.

Lorna picked it up. Its beauty fascinated her, but she didn't revere it as her husband did.

"And there are more of those, according to the story," Mannering murmured. "Still want a holiday in India?"

"In spite of what I read in the newspapers, yes."

"*What's* this?"

"I read all about the Rangipore jewels and the prince's quarrel and the fanatical group who say they'll get back all the jewels sold by Indian potentates for their private use. John – what more do you know?"

"I know I've a deceitful wife."

"About Phiroshah, and that thing, I mean."

Mannering winced.

"*Thing*? You're nearly a vandal." He dropped the banter. "I know only as much as you, but I guess that Phiroshah and probably some of the princes don't like your fanatics, the Indian authorities won't exert themselves, and Phiroshah thinks I might pull off a trick or two. I doubt if we know everything Phiroshah has in mind yet, and he'll only tell me all if I go to India."

"Then we'll go."

Mannering moved swiftly, took her into his arms and kissed her. He stood back and said quietly: "What's got into you?"

"You need a change desperately," Lorna said. "Some people would need a rest, but rest won't help you. You've had nothing to put your heart and soul into for too long. Quinns isn't enough by itself. Jewels are half of your life. And there's the conflict between the fleshpot princes and this organisation of zealots who seem to be working as the Baron's often worked – robbing to help the poor. But are they? Phiroshah's not a rogue. And you're more yourself since you first heard from him than you've been for weeks."

After a short silence Mannering said: "So that's it. Everything?"

"I *want* to see India," Lorna said.

He began to smile, kissed her again, and picked up the telephone.

"How long will it take you to be ready?"

"How long can I have?"

"I don't know." He had finished dialling, and said: "British

Overseas Airways? . . . Mr. David Kelly, please." He didn't hold on for long. "Hallo, David—John Mannering here . . . Fine, thanks, and thinking of flying to India on Saturday . . . Well, all right, Sunday would do . . . My dear chap, there must be room, there's only two of us." He laughed. "Yes, Lorna. Yes, I'll hold on a minute." He lowered the receiver. "Impossible for at least two weeks officially!" He put the receiver to his ear again, covering the mouthpiece with his hand. "There are two ways of tackling this. Go for Banu and any of his friends here. That might take some time, and would certainly run the risk of crossing Bristow. He's being very helpful. The other way is to fly to Bombay as soon as we can and get everything straight from Phiroshah."

"Do that," Lorna said.

"We've been able to fix it," Kelly said. "A couple of V.I.Ps. were going on Sunday, but they've been held up."

"I'll get Lorna to paint you one day. Where do I pick up the tickets? . . . Right. Thanks again. Here, hold on!" Lorna was waving frantically. "Just a minute."

"Ask him what the weather will be like at this time of the year, what clothes I'll need, all that kind of thing."

Mannering chuckled.

"David," he said. "Lorna wants to talk to you."

"*Thank* you, David," Lorna said a few minutes later. "You've been wonderful. 'Bye!" She rang off, eyes glowing. "We'll arrive during the monsoons, darling – the worst of the heat will be over. There'll be some rain, but it shouldn't be too bad. It'll be pretty warm everywhere, except at night if we go north. We needn't take too much in the way of clothes; we can always buy something there."

"Oh, always," said Mannering. "Dear David."

"Be enthusiastic, darling."

"Hurrah, hurrah, hurrah, we're going to Bombay in the morning! Well, on Sunday morning. Two days after Shani. I hope she isn't going to run into danger, but she seemed to think that will keep the diamond company. Better send it on ahead, I think."

"Yes, I'd do that." Lorna was suddenly sober.

Mannering laughed.

Lorna went off, with a host of things to do. Mannering picked up the telephone again and put in the call to Bombay; it would come through between four and five o'clock, he was told. He rang off and called a Golders Green number, where Sylvester, an old man who had once managed Quinns, lived in retirement. Could Sylvester come back for a month or two?

Sylvester not only could but seemed eager.

Mannering put down the receiver as Larraby came in, little the worse for wear. He had nothing new to report. Shani was at a small hotel where other Indians lived – some students, some politicians, some minor officials at India House.

Larraby was delighted to hear about Sylvester.

Mannering left just after one o'clock, had lunch at a snack bar, and then went to his flat at Green Street, Chelsea. Lorna wasn't there, and the maid was busy in the kitchen. There was a letter on the mat delivered by hand, not postmarked. He opened it as he went towards the bedrooms.

There were two words: "Don't go."

The maid knew nothing about it, or the note wouldn't have been on the mat. Mannering handled it gingerly to avoid smearing prints. The writing was in block capitals and offered no clue. He took it into his study, a small room furnished from Quinns, took out grey powder, a camel-hair brush and a sheet of paper. He tested the note. The only prints were his own.

He burned the note and cleared away all evidence of the test.

Lorna needn't know. Lorna was excited, and excitement dulled awareness of danger. No doubt she meant everything she said about him. No doubt she knew that months of inactivity had worn at his nerves; but above all that, she herself was eager to visit India and could blind herself to risk.

Already excitement was deep in Mannering, quickening his pulse and his mind.

He changed into an old suit and some worn golf shoes and left soon after two, carrying a Leica camera and a small make-up case.

At a lock-up garage near Victoria station he kept a Buick for emergencies he didn't want the police to know about.

There was a mirror on the wall. Locked inside, he opened the make-up case and started to work, to change himself. Deft touches at the eyes and mouth, rubber cheek pads, plastic covering for his teeth – these transformed him. It wasn't Mannering, but an older, plumper man who stared back at him from the mirror.

He slipped a specially made rubber ring round his waist and inflated it a little; his trousers buttoned tightly round it and increased the look of stoutness. He hadn't forgotten any tricks. He left the make-up case in the Buick, went out and took a taxi to the address which Plummer had given him, the address to which the man Banu had gone after following Shani.

The narrow street was filled with boarding-houses; several windows had a placard: "No vacancies". One opposite Banu's carried the sign: "Apartments".

A youngish fluffy-haired woman opened the door. She hadn't a front room, she was sorry. She saw the five pounds in his hand and changed her mind. She could put a bed up in her parlour to oblige the gentleman. He didn't want a bed, just an armchair by the window during the day and part of the evening. Oh, that was *easy*.

Yes, she was on the telephone.

Mannering talked to the exchange, arranged for the Bombay call to be put through here, and settled down to watch the boarding-house opposite. Banu came out once, and returned after twenty minutes, carrying a newspaper. Two or three other Indians arrived and went inside. Mannering smoked cigarette after cigarette, and the fluffy-haired woman kept bringing him cups of tea. It was nearly half-past four when a taxi drew up opposite, and Mannering had to change his position to see who got out.

It was the smaller of the two men who had raided the shop.

The man paid off the cab and hurried into the house. A few minutes later Mannering saw him at a first-floor window talking to Banu. The faces of both men registered vividly. Banu, youthful, lean, lithe and handsome, with the smooth good looks of the better-class Indian; the other man short, with an older face, ugly, teeth stained red from betel-nut chewing, a low wrinkled forehead. He wore a white turban, only a twist or two of cloth.

Mannering photographed them both, and other Indians who went to the house; better not to rely on memory.

Then the Bombay call came through.

Phiroshah's voice was as clear as if he were talking in the next room. It was frail, but his English was excellent. He was delighted to hear from Mannering, hoped that it meant that they would soon meet again. Yes? That was excellent news. His daughter Shani – yes, he would describe her. He described Shani in detail, and Mannering had no doubt that his daughter really had come to Quinns.

Mannering rang off and went back to the window seat. He could see two short words: "Don't go", as if they were painted on the window. Whoever had sent it had lost no time. Who *had* sent it? One of the Indians he'd seen? Banu?

Guessing didn't help. He had four days to clear everything up; couldn't afford to spend much time watching here; little for seeking the writer of the note. Had he been too hasty?

He concentrated on watching the doorway opposite. Now and again the camera clicked.

He was lighting a cigarette when a taxi drew up, just short of the boarding-house, and Shani stepped out.

CHAPTER SIX

THE FLIGHT

SHANI was in the house for over half an hour, but Mannering did not see her at any of the windows. When she appeared again, Banu was at the door to see her off. She did not look round at him, and he soon closed the door.

Mannering saw the girl's face clearly as she stepped into the waiting taxi. Her gravity, like the red sari, revealed nothing. As soon as she left, he went to the telephone and dialled the Chelsea flat.

Lorna answered.

"John, I wondered where—"

"Later," said Mannering, "over the celebrations. I haven't got used to that Louvre sale yet. My sweet, take an hour off from packing and preparing to pack and go to the Mirabar. Go right away, and you should be there about the time that Shani gets back. Tell her that we're going. Ask her whether she has been followed while in England, whether she's had any kind of trouble. Just that."

"Very well," said Lorna.

Mannering rang off.

He left the boarding-house and walked slowly towards the end of the street, limping. No one would have recognised him, and no one followed. He took a taxi to the garage, removed the make-up quickly, but still had traces of it when he took off the cushion and went to Chelsea. Lorna was out, so was the maid. Their bedroom was a glorious muddle. Lorna had started sorting out clothes in earnest. Leaving the room like this must have been a wrench.

It was half-past six.

Mannering bathed, got rid of the last traces of the make-up, dressed, and went into their bedroom. The flat was small but perfectly appointed, mostly furnished from Quinns. It was on one floor, with a large attic studio above for Lorna. He opened the wardrobe, knelt down, and pressed a small knob which revealed a secret drawer. Here were his tools. Any cracksman in England would have been proud of that set. Everything needed to force a safe was here – even nitroglycerin. He checked it, oiled some of the pieces, then packed everything in a small specially fitted case. It made a heavy parcel.

He took out two .32 pistols, several clips of ammunition, checked them, and put them away again.

It was seven o'clock.

He went up a step-ladder to the studio and looked round. One of Lorna's unfinished canvases stood on an easel – a portrait of a society beauty. Lorna's brush would be able to run riot in India.

He went down to the flat, and heard Lorna coming up the stairs. He stood in front of the door as she opened it. She started.

"Oh!" She recovered. "Brute!"

"Just testing your nerve," said Mannering. She wore the same clothes as she had that morning; her cheeks were flushed; excitement hadn't dimmed in her eyes. He took her hands and pulled her to him. She was breathless when he let her go.

Her eyes were radiant.

"Still like that?"

"Just like that."

"These Indian women are very beautiful."

"Every man to his taste. How's Shani tonight?"

"Solemn as ever."

"What did she have to say?"

"She was gravely delighted, said that she would cable her father immediately and that she was sure that you would succeed."

"Ah," said Mannering. "And the rest?"

"She hasn't been followed, at least she doesn't think she has. I'd say she was completely innocent."

"That's because you're so young," said Mannering. "Did she happen to mention that she had been visiting compatriots this evening?"

Lorna didn't speak.

"And that she had a session with a man named Banu, who had an earlier session with the man who escaped from the shop."

Lorna said weakly: "I don't believe it."

"Of course, it might have been an innocent visit; she may know nothing about Banu," Mannering said drily. "He might even be the man her father sent to look after her, and he also could be the rogue."

"It's hard to believe that girl—"

"I don't know what will happen to you when you meet a really handsome Indian prince," said Mannering. "It's time to dress, we're going to Ciro's for champagne and—"

"We are *not*," said Lorna. "We're going to have supper in the kitchen. There's far too much to do to go gadding about at night."

Mannering left her in the kitchen when the telephone bell rang. He picked up the receiver in his small, book-lined study, still smiling at Lorna's eagerness.

"John Mannering here."

A man spoke in a soft, penetrating voice.

"Don't go," he said. "Don't go."

The line went dead as the smile faded from Mannering's lips. Lorna called: "Who was it?" and his "Wrong number" rang true. He was at his gayest at supper.

The consequence of the evening's earnest inspection of wardrobes was that Lorna would have to do some shopping next day.

Mannering left the flat soon after breakfast. To prove his eagerness old Sylvester was already with Larraby in the shop. Mannering took the blue diamond from the strong-room, where Larraby had put it for the night, slipped it into a pad of cotton wool and then into a wash-leather bag, and went out. By ten o'clock he was at a small diamond merchant's office and workshop in Hatton Gardens. Gall, the diamond merchant, was a little old man with wispy grey hair and a wealth of knowledge about jewels. Little surprised him. Mannering simply took the diamond out of the cotton wool and handed it across.

"Can you make a copy of that for me quickly?"

Gall caught his breath, touched the stone, then picked it up between a pair of tweezers. He took it to the bright light above his desk, sat down slowly, an inspected it. He seemed to take an age. Finished, he laid it down reverently on the pad of cotton wool.

"Beaut-i-ful," he declared.

"Can you copy it?"

"Oh yes, yes. But not perfectly, Mr. Mannering, and not well. You know that. We can put some life into white diamonds, even into rose tints, but this—I have never seen anything like it. What a remarkable man you are."

"How would you value it?" Mannering asked.

"Value?" Gall gave a little laugh. "You know as well as I do, it is worth everything a man can be persuaded to pay for it. If it were mine, I should have to be hard up indeed if I sold it for less than ten thousand pounds. I might hold out for twenty. I think I would get it. More, even. To the collector who really wants it there is no price. You're very wise to have a copy; you mustn't take risks with it."

"No," said Mannering solemnly. "When can I have a copy?"

"Tomorrow morning."

"Thank you. If you'll take the photo and measurements, I'll take it away with me."

"Yes, please do that. *Please.* I would prefer not to have it here." Gall busied himself with calipers, pencil and paper, and kept muttering to himself, occasionally stopping to look at the stone for its own sake.

Mannering left just after eleven, with the diamond in his pocket. He wasn't followed. He had seldom been more conscious of the possibility of being shadowed; he doubled on his own tracks, and was as thorough as if he were being trailed by the police.

He saw no sign of trouble.

He went to Whitehall, saw friends, made arrangements to take the stone out of the country, and went to the flat. It was then nearly one o'clock, but Lorna was still out. There was no other message, but "Don't go" hammered against his mind. He telephoned Shani. She was in. She hadn't been out that day; she didn't think that she would be going out at all. She had to leave early tomorrow for the airport.

Mannering followed her next morning to the airport. He was made-up and unrecognisable. She had two Indians with her, neither of the men he'd seen before. They had no difficulty with the Customs, and boarded the plane among the forty-odd passengers. The only really colourful note was Shani's red sari; it gave her added gravity, put perfection to her beauty. She disappeared inside the aircraft, and Mannering waited until it taxied towards the runway and took off.

At Quinns, Sylvester and Larraby were like two old cronies and almost impatient for Mannering to leave them in charge.

Mannering, half-asleep, heard Lorna moving about, heard the bedroom door open and close, lay still until she came back. He watched her through his lashes. It was early – a little after six o'clock. She hadn't made up, her hair was set, but she looked good as she put a tea tray on the bedside table. She wore a dressing-gown and nothing else.

"Darling! Time to wake up."

Mannering kept his eyes closed.

She touched his shoulder. "Wake up! Today's the day, and we mustn't be late."

Mannering opened one eye.

"I've never known you so considerate," he said. "Where's my tea?"

"Here. Don't be too long, because—"

"I know, I know. There isn't time." He sat up, and she drank one cup of tea hurriedly and went out; he heard the bath water running. He finished his tea leisurely, went into the bathroom and shaved while she bathed. He flung her a towel and watched her get out – and chuckled, from the joy of it.

They were ready three-quarters of an hour before time.

Lorna had been to her parents' home in Hertfordshire the night before; there were no goodbyes today. She sat on the arm of a chair impatiently.

"We could start walking," said Mannering amiably.

"Brute."

"Or go for half an hour's drive through the country; you'll probably long for green fields and leafy trees when you're in India."

Lorna jumped up.

"Let's go, now!"

Most of their luggage was at the airport. Mannering carried a pigskin bag which they would want on the journey, and a brief-case. There was a sealed packet in the brief-case; Lorna didn't ask what was in it.

Two Indians were at the airport when they arrived.

They were in the Customs office, when Mannering talked earnestly to a clerk, opened the brief-case, handed over the package which had been officially sealed by the London office. The clerk marked it again and handed it back. Mannering stored it away in the brief-case and locked it, then, with Lorna holding his arm, walked to the waiting-room. Their plane, a Britannia, was warming up. Mechanics were standing about beneath the wings, near the fuel pump; chocks were in position. No one seemed to be in a hurry. It was a clear morning, with only a few high, fleecy clouds.

The Indians stood by, apparently taking no special notice of the Mannerings.

The loudspeaker blared.

"Passengers for Karachi and further east, please make your way towards the aircraft on your left. Please put out your cigarettes before leaving the building, and do not smoke again until you are advised by your stewardess. Passengers for Karachi and further east . . ."

The Mannerings led the little crowd, people they didn't know at all but some of whom they would know well before the next three days were out. There were more men than women. One couple was young; obvious honeymooners, delighted with each other. A middle-aged woman was dressed in the height of fashion, made up superbly; most of the men noticed her.

The two Indians were last in the line.

A messenger came hurrying as Mannering stepped on to the gangway leading into the aircraft.

"Mr. Mannering?"

"Yes."

"Some telegrams, sir."

"Oh, thanks." There were four. Mannering took them and went in. The stewardess looked at their tickets and led them to their seats; the wings didn't hide the view. There were moments of bustle, then the doors were closed. Lighted signs over the pilot's cabin read: *Fasten belts. No smoking.*

Ten minutes of warming up and of taxi-ing, then a deep-throated roar from the four engines. They raced along the runway.

They were airborne!

The Mannerings watched the countryside first flashing then crawling by and the earth gradually getting further away. Two stewardesses stood together near the pilot's cabin, with bundles of newspapers under their arms and a dish of barley sugar. They started to hand out papers and sweets.

The ground seemed a long way off.

The two Indians sat together at the back of the plane, six seats behind the Mannerings.

"Nothing's happened," Lorna said.

"Yet." Mannering began to open the telegrams; one was from Lorna's mother and father, one from Larraby and Sylvester, the third from Bristow. He chuckled. "Good old Bill." Lorna was attracted by something she saw below, and he opened the fourth telegram. It read: "Don't go."

Lorna didn't see him screw it up and drop it under his seat. The engines throbbed the same grim warning note:

"Don't go, don't go."

CHAPTER SEVEN

BOMBAY

"EXPECTATIONS fulfilled?" asked Mannering.

There had been some running repairs to the aircraft, and they had been out into the streets of Karachi; into the heat, the colour and the filth, the squalor and the beauty. Mannering could see it all mirrored in Lorna's eyes; a blurred picture, because neither eyes nor mind had been able to accept everything, and the conscious mind had rejected much.

"Well?" asked Mannering as they climbed into the aircraft.

"I suppose so." Lorna sounded as confused and numbed as she looked. She looked out of the small, round window, as his gaze fell on the envelope tucked by the side of his seat. Sight of it would have burst the bubble of Lorna's fascination.

He sat down, slid it out, then went to the back of the plane, where the magazines were kept. He opened the envelope.

There was a change of phrasing. This said: "Go back."

Lorna still did not know about the campaign of letters, but sooner or later she would have to. He joined her, and she turned to glance at him, then looked back at the Indian mechanics moving towards the airport buildings. Europeans were out-numbered six or seven to one. Two or three white-faced people stood with a group of Indians, the women all dressed in gaily coloured saris, to watch the plane take off. Lorna waited until the figures were tiny dots against the brown earth, then turned to Mannering and rested her head against the back of the seat.

"I keep seeing camels," she said. "Chasing me."

"I keep seeing yashmaks."

"And wondering what's beneath them," said Lorna. "I'd heard so much about it, but the reality is—" She paused.

"So much better and so much worse?"

"Well, perhaps," said Lorna.

"And no robbers," murmured Mannering.

Lorna glanced down at the brief-case, which was against the wall, between her knees and the side. She laughed.

"I think that was all a dream."

"And when we get to Bombay, we'll find Phiroshah's sons alive again and Shani just a vision! I'm going to sleep," finished Mannering.

When he opened his eyes, half an hour afterwards, they were flying through cloudless sky towards Bombay; and Lorna was sketching, with a pad on her knee, a far-away look in her eyes. She had put several sheets aside; on each was the head of a camel. Mannering grinned. She glanced sideways.

"I can't help it," she said defensively. "They fascinated me. It isn't as if I hadn't seen them before, but they're like big overgrown horses with a hump and a sneer."

"I didn't mind bringing you to paint the Taj Mahal, but when it comes to camels—. You'll change. Cigarette?"

"Not now."

"Wait until you see Phiroshah," Mannering said. "You'll find your fingers itching for a pencil."

None of this was quite real. The flight, the smoothness, the bright sun, the blue sky, the dry, yellowy land beneath; the distant sea. Life had changed. All pressure, all fears, all sense of urgency had gone – but for that curt: "Go back". Even the brief-case was part of a dream, a faint reminder of what might come and what had been. Reality was within the aircraft; the stewardesses, now in their white uniforms; the crew, also in white – seven altogether – the passengers. They knew all the passengers except three, who had kept themselves very much to themselves. The Indians were boys – happy boys who had been educated in England and were anxious to get home. They spoke excellent English, much more pure than most of the passengers. Everyone liked them. No one could be less sinister.

But someone had put that note there.

The stewardess brought round tea . . . dinner. It grew dark. Because of the delay, they were to land by night. Now and again they looked out of the windows and saw lights below; seldom many lights. Two or three large cities spread the radiance out for some distance. Mostly they were villages and lights were yellow glimmers. They flew over the unknown which tomorrow would become reality.

They dozed.

Mannering felt the stewardess touch his shoulder.

"Better wake up, Mr. Mannering, we're nearly there."

Lorna started up. "*There*?"

"In about twenty minutes." The stewardess went on to the passengers behind them. Lorna began to pack their oddments in the pigskin bag. Mannering filled his pockets, slipped some books into the brief-case. Soon, the lights appeared; a myriad of lights, shining on – what?

The signs flashed on. *Fasten belts. No smoking.*

"*Now* I'm really beginning to believe it," said Lorna.

The aircraft tipped to one side and shuddered once or twice; gave passengers the queasy uneasiness which came with landing and taking off. Only the drone of the engines sounded. They were curving round. The Mannerings' window overlooked the city and the lights – lights of all colours. There was one great arc of them, with blackness in the middle. The man behind said:

"That's the Queen's Necklace."

"Queen's Necklace?"

"The lights round the Marine Drive," the passenger said. "You'll see. Beautiful. Deceptively beautiful." He was a cynical English globe-trotter and an engineer. "I hate the place."

An American alongside them called: "Don't put them off, they'll just love it."

The flares of the airport showed up; they were flying inland. Again, the only sound was of the droning engines; these seemed louder. Go back, go back. Flares were a long way off one moment, then seemed alongside. They felt the wheels touch ground. A woman at the back laughed, to relieve her own and others' tension. Lorna squeezed Mannering's hand.

Shadowy figures appeared, the passengers stood up, laughing and talking. They began to file off the aircraft. The American joined them as they reached the ground.

"You're *the* Mannering, aren't you? John Mannering."

Mannering laughed. "Jewels."

"That's right. On business?"

"Lord, no. Hol—I mean, vacation!"

"Have a good time." The American went swinging off into the darkness and the airport buildings. They knew he was on some kind of special mission, and would be hustled through Customs. They had been warned that Indian Customs were thorough. They were philosophic. Two other passengers joined them; somehow Mannering and Lorna were parted. Dark-faced men were on either side – porters, coolies. Mannering carried his brief-case, Lorna the pigskin. He could hear Lorna laughingly promising to give a French passenger a sketch which she had made of her.

There was a smell; not offensive, but different, spicy.

"It's a great country," a man said. "You'll love it or you'll hate it. I hate it!" He offered Mannering a cigarette as they neared the door. Lights glowed from the waiting-room and the other buildings. White-clad Indians were waiting for their employers. People bustled. A little gang of small children had found their way on to the airfield and gathered round, begging. Officials cuffed and cursed them. Mannering's hand went to his pocket.

"I shouldn't," a passenger said. "If you start that, you'll be at it all the time."

"Sahib, ver' 'ongry, ver' 'ongry." A little chap, coming hardly up to Mannering's waist, stood in front of him. Light fell on a pale, coffee-coloured face; on curly hair that looked verminous; on a plump chest and overblown stomach; the lad wore only a loincloth. He rubbed his stomach swiftly, mechanically. "Sahib, ver' 'ongry."

"I *shouldn't*," the passenger began.

The boy jumped at Mannering and punched him in the stomach

viciously; there was more strength in the punch than in most men's. Mannering staggered back, gasping with pain. He felt a clutching hand at his right wrist, then more pain as his wrist was wrenched. His fingers released the brief-case. He felt it go, saw the boy race into the darkness of the aerodrome. Officials gave chase, passengers shouted, Mannering regained his balance and pressed a hand against his stomach. Officials surrounded him, all talking at once; only one had any English. Lorna was suddenly at his side.

"Damned thieving scoundrels!" one passenger was shouting. Go get them—don't stand round *here.*"

"Anything valuable, Mannering?" asked another.

Mannering felt physically sick enough to be silent. Lorna answered for him – yes. In fact, there was the replica of the blue diamond and some books. Two men helped Mannering into the waiting-room. He didn't really need help. He felt sick and it was hot – and he could no longer escape reality. There was turmoil as he went through the Customs, picked out ahead of the others. Only by being imperious did Lorna manage to keep him company. An official who spoke good English questioned him with almost suspicious closeness. What had been in the brief-case ? A complete list of the contents, please. He handed over sheets of paper, as well as long, printed questionnaires. He ignored Lorna; he would ignore all women. It was fiercely hot in here, and the odour was more pronounced.

Mannering filled in his forms and signed them; Lorna did the same. They were asked to wait, while the official disappeared, darkly suspicious. Mannering sat in an easy chair, with two khaki-clad officials who might be soldiers or police by the door; guards. Mannering lit a cigarette.

"Nice start," he said.

"What on earth does the fellow think you did?"

"He suspects the worst. Neat way to smuggle, having someone laid on to steal your bag."

"The fool!"

"No respect for women," grinned Mannering. "No equality here, my sweet. I wonder—"

The door opened. The suspicious official, a stern and severe figure until then, came in first. He was all smiles. He was fat and looked ridiculous in his uniform, and his teeth were stained red. Behind him came a little wizened figure, a Gandhi of a figure, dressed in a white wrap and white dhoti. His skinny legs were nut-brown. His feet were big, and he wore open sandals. There was a smile on his face which touched his eyes, and made one forget how old he looked.

"My dear friend Mannering!" He held out a hand, European fashion. "And your wife. We are honoured—greatly honoured." He smiled at Lorna and bowed. "I am Aly Phiroshah, Mrs. Mannering."

He looked a saint.

Lorna said: "How do you do," and felt foolish.

Mannering said: "Is it good to see you!"

"I am sorry you have had such an unfortunate start. You will tell me about it afterwards – I have a car waiting outside." Phiroshah smiled at the official, who snatched up Lorna's pigskin bag and carried it for her to the door, into the warmth of the evening. The stars were shining and there was crystal beauty in the heavens.

A Daimler with a chauffeur standing by the door was near the Customs building.

"Mrs. Mannering first, please." Phiroshah climbed in after her, Mannering followed. The official, still all smiles, handed in the bag, bowed, closed the door. The chauffeur opened the door and closed it again to his own satisfaction.

"Welcome—doubly welcome," said Phiroshah. "I do not know what you have in mind to do, Mr. Mannering, but for the first few days you had better stay here in Bombay. I have seen the suite reserved for you at the Taj Mahal Hotel. You will also use my house as if it were your own, but in the beginning you will be happier at the hotel. You will have the opportunity to adjust yourselves. We will talk later. You will wish to look about you."

He had made sure that they had window seats, and he was in the middle. He must have been told of the incident at the airport, but hadn't referred to it. They looked out of the windows into a new world.

They went through narrow streets with shops open on either side

– only a shop here and there, but it was nearly one o'clock in the morning. Dhoti-clad figures squatted at the shop entrances. Flares burned – mostly old-fashioned napthalene flares or candles, with here and there an electric light. The sidewalks were crowded. Small men and small women walked to and fro, some with children. There were long bundles of rags on the pavement and in the gutter. People stepped over them indifferently. A bundle stirred; a man's head appeared, then a hand; the hand clutched the blanket and pulled it over the head, and the blanket became a bundle of rags again.

"It is not all like this," said Phiroshah.

They sat and watched – and Mannering found his mind numbed. Just tiredness? He gave up trying to think of it.

They passed tall, white modern buildings, and others with onion-shaped domes, black against the stars. Everywhere, the bundles of rags were on the sidewalk and in the gutters. Little stalls were filled with foodstuffs they didn't recognise. The Daimler purred along, made several turnings once they had reached the heart of the city, then drew up outside an imposing building. Opposite was the harbour, and the stars glistened on the unruffled surface of the water.

"I shall come to your room with you, and then leave you," Phiroshah said. "There is time to talk tomorrow." He smiled. "Thank you for the diamond, which was delivered to me by the airline officials to whom you wisely entrusted it. We shall perhaps find your brief-case."

Mannering said: "The diamond could have been in it."

The smile deepened.

"I do not believe that you would have carried it in such a careless way, my friend. I am not troubled."

They climbed out. A dozen small boys rushed to them, begging alms. Phiroshah said something in their own tongue, and they backed away. Servants came out – four of them, all dressed in white.

The entrance was spacious, the lift smooth. They were on the third floor, where the passages were wide and there was an atmosphere of luxury. Phiroshah led the way, his little legs moving two steps to their one. He turned a corner. Two white-clad men, turbanned, dark-faced, stood at attention outside a door.

"These are your two boys," Phiroshah said. "You will find them useful. The taller is Amu, the shorter you will call Joseph. They are both Christians, I thought that wise. Catholics, perhaps, I should add. Amu!"

The taller "boy" turned and opened the door. Mannering glanced at him once, looked away, studied him more closely. He went with Lorna into the outer room of the suite, which was furnished as one might be in any European luxury hotel. Doors led to the right and left.

"Amu's English is better than Joseph's," said Phiroshah. "He is intelligent, too. Don't worry about anything for the first few hours, please. I wish you good night." He bowed, without attempting to shake hands, turned and went out. Mannering and Lorna stood together, watching him.

Amu approached and bowed.

Amu, the bearer, had called at the London boarding-house where Banu had stayed. Mannering had a photograph of him.

CHAPTER EIGHT

AMU THE SERVANT

AMU'S English was good, his voice soft.

"If the sahib or memsahib require anything, I shall obtain it."

"Thank you. Anything, darling?"

"Just sleep," said Lorna.

"We'll go to bed," said Mannering. "Don't call us in the morning, Amu."

"Very good, sahib. This way, please."

The bedroom was vast; there were twin beds, brocaded easy chairs and a couch; everything resplendent. Doors leading off led on one side to a bathroom, on the other to a dressing-room. Amu guided them gravely from one to the other, went to the door and bowed himself out. Mannering and Lorna stood together at the foot of the beds; and Lorna laughed. It was a little shrill.

"Fantasy!"

"Just India," said Mannering. "Feel like a bath?"

"I couldn't." Her eyes looked heavy with tiredness, although they were so bright. "That boy who took—"

"Tomorrow," said Mannering firmly.

Their nightclothes were in the pigskin bag. Lorna was in bed within ten minutes. Mannering went into the bathroom, leaving the door open; he could see the main door from there. He smoked a cigarette as he ran the bath-water; that would reassure Lorna. When he went back to the bedroom, Lorna was sleeping. He went to the door and locked it. There were two bolts, and he shot them. He went to the dressing-room, where a door led to a balcony. He locked both the balcony and dressing-room doors. There were no windows and only the one door into the bathroom. There was no need to lock anything there. He went and sat down on an armchair and looked at Lorna and contemplated the main bedroom door.

Amu would be in the suite.

Amu had been in London a week ago; Amu, or someone so like him that Mannering had been deceived. He took the photographs from a travel-fold in the pigskin case, studied one, and was quite convinced; it was either of Amu or his double.

Phiroshah had taught him a lesson; the direct approach was the good approach here. He felt tired, but doubted if he would sleep. He got into bed and lay on his back, with only the bed light on. At last he turned and switched it off and settled down.

"Darling," Lorna said.

Mannering stirred.

"Darling."

Mannering blinked.

"Why did you bolt the doors?"

Mannering sat up with a start.

"Do what?"

"Bolt the doors."

"Oh, that," said Mannering. "I felt nervous. It's the first time I've been robbed like that."

"Just nerves?"

"I'm a bundle of them," he said, and grinned. She was sitting up in bed, hugging her knees. She wore a nylon nightdress because they were easy to wash and she might be roughing it. He decided in favour of nylon nightdresses. He had slept with only a sheet over him; and even that made him feel too warm. He pushed it back.

"They were certainly waiting for us," Lorna said. "Did you expect it?"

"The way of it surprised me," Mannering said.

"Do you wish we hadn't come?"

"Not yet!"

There was a spell of silence.

Then: "It's hot," said Lorna. "Is there a balcony?"

"Oh yes."

"And do we get tea if we want it?"

"We're at the Taj Mahal Hotel, and we get everything," said Mannering. "Personally, I'm going to have fruit juice." He got out of bed, unbolted the door and turned the key, and looked outside. Joseph stood by the outer door; Amu wasn't in sight.

"Good morning, Joseph."

"Good morning, sahib."

"Orange juice and tea, please."

"Yes, sahib."

"Where is Amu?"

"Amu is pressing the sahib's clothes." There wasn't much the matter with Joseph's English.

"All right. We'll be on the balcony."

"Very good, sahib."

Lorna, with a light scarf round her shoulders, was on the balcony. The harbour was calm, the morning sun sparkled on it like diamonds. Yachts at anchor to their left rose and fell gently. Almost in front of them was the massive stonework of the Gateway of India. Beggars and pedlars and tourists were already there; two women were taking photographs. A gharry with a sorrowful-looking horse and a fat driver stood waiting for them. Most of the Indians who passed were men; and most wore dhotis, some with a linen jacket over them, others with the ample folds of muslin. Now and again a woman in a bright sari passed.

Joseph brought in tea and orange juice for two.

"We'll breakfast up here," said Mannering.

"Very good, sahib." Joseph paused. "When the sahib is ready, please say. I will bring him."

Mannering looked puzzled. "Bring who?"

"There is a man desiring to speak."

"Oh," said Mannering. "English?"

"No, sahib."

"What's his name?"

"He gives no name."

"How long has he been here?" asked Lorna.

"Two hours," said Joseph. "He will not go; he will wait if needs be, all day."

It was half-past ten.

Mannering said: "Tell him I won't see him."

"Very good, sahib."

Lorna looked her protest, but waited until Joseph had gone.

"You don't know who he is or what he wants."

Mannering smiled. "If he's Indian, he won't go away because of a first refusal, and he'll probably send in a little more information about himself. Tea or orange juice?"

"Tea," said Lorna.

Joseph came back in ten minutes with a card. He handed it to Mannering and stood back. The card was printed in English, and announced that Mr. I. Patandi, of Bombay, was a dealer in books in all languages, ancient and modern. There was a message scribbled in a bold, boyish hand.

"Please, Mr. Mannering, most important. Not business only."

"Is this the man who's been waiting?"

"Yes, sahib."

"Has Amu seen him?"

"Amu sent him away. He would not go."

"I see," said Mannering. "All right. Tell him I'll see him for five minutes, between now and one o'clock. I can't be sure what time. And I'm not interested in business."

"Please," said Joseph. "What did the sahib say?"

Amu appeared at the doorway of the balcony, spoke swiftly to the other boy in Hindi, advanced a step, apologised to Mannering because he had not been on duty when the sahib and memsahib had woken. He understood the message and would tell the man. He went out.

"John," said Lorna. "Aren't you being a bit high-handed? India belongs to the Indians now."

"I can't imagine what Mr. Patandi wants, but we'll find out whether he's eager enough to wait for another two hours,"

Mannering said. "Probably he wants to sell us books, in spite of the 'not business only'."

"I suppose nothing I say will change you. He's very good-looking, isn't he?"

"Patandi? Haven't seen the chap."

"Amu."

"Oh, there are hundreds like him," said Mannering. "Don't start seeing every face on canvas. Wait until you've had a good survey."

"Or stick to camels," said Lorna. "I've said it for you. John, why did you lock and bolt the doors?"

He didn't joke, and didn't explain.

"I think it's a good thing to start. We ought to do it everywhere, like locking a car door. We might forget when it really matters, otherwise."

She wasn't wholly satisfied but accepted the answer, finished her tea and brushed her forehead.

"Sticky?" asked Mannering.

"Don't be ridiculous. Tea's a cooling drink, after the first few minutes."

Mannering grimaced at her.

"Don't keep Patandi waiting too long," pleaded Lorna, as she got up. "I'm anxious to see what he looks like."

They had bathed and finished breakfast by half-past eleven. The only coolness was in the rooms, and there it was illusory, the big fans stirring the hot air. Outside, it was roasting hot; or boiling hot, humid enough to make them sticky after any slight movement. Amu and Joseph had waited on them in a style which was barely remembered in England; they were silent and efficient.

At twenty-five to twelve Mannering rang a small handbell and Amu appeared almost on the instant.

"Is Patandi still there, Amu?"

"Yes, sahib."

"We'll see him," said Mannering.

"Very good, sahib." The "sahib" always came after the shortest phrase. Amu went out. Lorna dabbed a little powder on her nose.

Both were pretending to look towards the open door which led to the balcony when Mr. I. Patandi came in.

They did not pretend for long.

Patandi was a big man; not only fat, but tall, six foot three or four, Mannering judged. He wore a dhoti, and the thick calves of his brown legs stuck out from it. His sandals had rope soles. He wore a little black turban and carried a brief-case.

It was Mannering's brief-case.

CHAPTER NINE

THE GARRULOUS BOOKSELLER

"GENTLEMAN!" cried Patandi. "Lady!" He bowed, and the brief-case swung in front of him. "You are goodness itself to spare me your good time. Thank you." He straightened up and beamed at them. Lorna sat absolutely still, looking at the case. Mannering appeared not to notice the case, and murmured: "Five minutes is all I can manage, I'm afraid."

"I understand, and it is sufficient. I thank you for it." Patandi held tightly on to the brief-case. "I welcome you to wonderful India. It is your first visit, yes? Yes!" He nodded vigorously. "Such a wonderful place, so much beauty, I can show you everything. Everything. I, Patandi, am the best guide in all India. Yes?"

"Probably," said Mannering mildly.

"You will find out I talk only the truth," said Patandi. "Yes. Such a famous man and famous lady, they must see only everything of the best. I show it to them." He leaned forward and breathed aniseed into Mannering's face. "I show it better than any guide in India. My English, it is perfect. Years ago I was a guide, now I am a bookseller, selling only the best books. But I have assistants – they can sell books; I have more important work to do."

"You're very good, but—"

"And cheap!" cried Patandi. "So cheap you don't know. I show you Indian rope trick. Elephant walking over man. Sensational things only. Things very few white people see. You have just and only one week; that is time enough for me to show you – if you fly. You are not afraid to fly? To see India in one week, it is ridiculous, unless you fly. Taj Mahal, the forts, mosques, everything. Himalayas? Darjeeling? Yes, it can all be done in one week, everything. I, Patandi, say so."

"We may be here longer," said Mannering.

Patandi frowned. Patandi frowning was a sight to see. He leaned forward and tapped Mannering's shoulder confidentially. His teeth looked good, but were stained red from chewing betel nut, and the aniseed was thick on his breath. His eyes were dark as olives, and intent and serious.

"You have one week." He lowered his voice. "No more. After that, you go. Gentleman, I look at you when I come in. In one minute I say to myself, this is a very wise gentleman. Like all the English. *Very* wise. One week, and it is enough. One week, and this English gentleman who is famous – and famous lady also – will know he wishes no more to see in India. Too dirty. Smelly. Not for famous English gentleman. And lady. One week, that is *all*, Mr. Mannering."

He squeezed Mannering's shoulder.

"I may want to stay a month. Two months."

Patandi shook his head. No one could mistake his earnestness.

"One week *only*, gentleman. That is final. Understand, India is unhealthy place. Smallpox. Cholera. Everything!" He narrowed his eyes. "Dacoits. You know dacoits? Armed robbers, so!" He made a gesture with his hand; the fingers clenched as if holding the handle of a knife, the thrust towards Mannering's stomach. Lorna exclaimed involuntarily. Patandi turned, unimpeded by his bulk, bowed and looked the picture of consternation and remorse.

"Famous lady, I am very sorry, I did not wish to alarm you. Ridiculous. I only tell you what can happen in India. Yes. India . . ." He clutched Lorna's shoulder and leaned towards her. "Old India good, new India bad. In old India, Europeans and English safe. I, Patandi, am great friend of the English. I hate to see them go, but— no politician. If a politician—" He drew back, then up to his great height, held his head back, then with a swift movement ran his forefinger across his throat and made a choking noise.

Lorna was pale.

Patandi bobbed his head forward again and beamed.

"Old India good for English people, Americans, everyone. New India, *very* bad. Not safe. Safe with Patandi for one week only. I regret, after that I must sell my books. The fools I leave to sell them for me will charge half the price or run away with all the money. You see the great sacrifice I make for you?"

He beamed like a happy child.

"Yes, I see," said Mannering. "Let me think about it, Patandi. Where can I find you?"

Patandi was proud.

"My shops," he announced. "Everywhere. Good books, ancient and modern. I have seven and there are also Greek. *In* Greek. Many Latin. All Indian cultures, also. I do everything, but you have only one week in India, so I give it all up."

He turned a bow into a salaam and brought the brief-case between his knees. Straightening up, he looked at it as if surprised at seeing it, and then his eyes widened and glowed and he held the case out to Mannering, as a magician might present a rabbit.

"Famous Mr. Mannering, this is *yours.*"

Mannering said: "That's right."

"Where did you get it?" Lorna demanded sharply.

"Lady, ask no questions, hear no lies," said Patandi, and roared with laughter. "I tell you. These boys, they will beg, rob, steal, do anything, yes. They climb through to the airfield, they attack last night, isn't that so? They take the case to the old man who employs them. A bad old man, yes. He sends it with a boy to me. You ask, why to me? I tell you. I sell many things. Bags, cases – very fine lady's crocodile, tiger-skin handbags, lady, best in India; you must come and see for yourself, please. New, second-hand. I pay twenty rupees for this bag, the boy goes, I open it—and what do I find? Your name, Mr. Mannering. So, I am an honest man. Twenty rupees – what is it? The price of honour? Too cheap. I give it back to you."

He held the case on the palms of his hands and thrust it in front of Mannering. His smile was gentle now, as if appealing for praise. Mannering, who had looked at him throughout the last ten minutes with dull eyes and without moving, took it and smiled thinly.

"Very kind of you. Thanks."

"Sir, it is my duty," said Patandi. "An honest man returns to its rightful owner any article which strays into his possession. Not all poor men are dishonest. When will you come to see me?"

"This afternoon."

"Come to any of my shops, say you wish to see me, they will send for me at once. Five minutes, ten minutes, and I will be with you. Famous English gentleman, *au revoir.*" He turned massively, then darted a glance at Lorna. "And famous lady."

He reached the door.

It opened, and Amu appeared, looking at Patandi with sneering contempt. Patandi stalked out. Amu closed the door silently. Mannering sat without moving. Lorna lit a cigarette, stood up and began to walk restlessly about the room. She started to speak, looked at him and stopped.

He picked up the brief-case, opened it deliberately, and took out the contents. From one section, three novels; from another, two slim volumes of Browning and Keats; from the third, a package which looked like a book. He opened this. There were no leaves, but a small, sealed brown paper packet was inside. The seal had been neatly broken, as neatly re-joined. Lorna moved towards him and rested a hand on his shoulder as she looked down. He unwrapped the package and came to a thick cardboard box, opened this to the cotton wool, pulled the cotton wool aside, and found a blue diamond.

It was the replica that Gall had made for him.

The surface was scratched and he peered at it closely, then took a small magnifying lens out of his pocket and peered through it. He gave a quick, gusty laugh.

"What is it?" Lorna demanded.

"They're good. They're very good." He handed her the glass and the paste diamond. After a pause, she read out slowly: *"Go back."*

She lowered the glass.

"We can have a week of sightseeing and then we have to go back," murmured Mannering. "Orders."

"I think I'm going to be frightened," Lorna said. "There was a note on your seat at Karachi, wasn't there?"

"And I thought I'd fooled you!"

"What did it say?"

" 'Go back'."

"Had there been anything else?"

"A series of cryptic orders not to come."

"Why didn't you tell me?"

"You weren't in a mood to heed the instruction. Nor was I." Mannering leaned back and stretched out his legs, lit a cigarette, and looked at Lorna. Her nose was a little shiny, and there was perspiration at her eyelids; neither stopped her from looking lovely, and uncertainty had put a new, provocative light into her eyes. "The case was snatched at the airfield because they hoped the real diamond would be in it, but there were side-issues. The small boy could have used a knife as easily as he used his fist, so I know what to expect. Patandi comes and allows me a week. If I stay longer, there will be trouble – worse trouble than at the airport. Clever Patandi."

Lorna said: "He could be a devil."

"Oh yes. He wrapped the threat up beautifully so that we knew what he meant and yet it could be taken so innocently." Mannering chuckled. "I suppose we ought to be thankful that they've given us a week's grace."

"What are you going to do?"

"Have a heart-to-heart talk with old Phiro while you see the sights of Bombay," said Mannering. He rang the hand bell, and Amu appeared, like a spirit at the rub of a lamp.

"Memsahib will have a drive round the city," Mannering said. "You'll go with her, Amu."

"Yes, sahib."

"I am going to see Mr. Phiroshah."

"Mr. Phiroshah, sahib, will come to see you at noon, if that is convenient."

"Just right," said Mannering. "Get a taxi and—"

"The car is waiting, with Mr. Phiroshah's chauffeur."

"Better," said Mannering appreciatively.

He stood on the steps of the hotel, watching Lorna being driven off. Amu sat in front, next to the driver. The excitement was back in Lorna's eyes; he hadn't thought that Patandi would drive it away for long. The threat hadn't yet become imminent. He lit a cigarette and strolled across the road, walked through the Gateway of India, with boys rubbing their stomachs in front of him, old men selling foreign stamps, others selling postcards. A brisk youth in European clothes and carrying a Gladstone bag saluted smartly as Mannering leaned against the parapet and looked out at the harbour and the small yachts.

"Cut corns, mister? Fully qualified chiropodist, mister."

Mannering grinned. "No corns, thanks."

"Stop corns coming, mister. Fully qualified chiropodist. Very cheap."

"No, thanks."

The youth drew nearer and lowered his voice.

"Dirty postcards, mister; very cheap. They—"

A soft voice sounded nearby, two or three words which had an electrifying effect on the qualified chiropodist. He tucked the postcards away and hurried off, while Phiroshah, dressed exactly as he had been the night before and with the sun making his dhoti look snowy-white, smiled up at Mannering. Mannering, in light-grey tropicals, was more than a head taller.

"Good morning, my friend. You will have to learn the few words that will show them you're not just another tourist."

"Good morning," said Mannering. 'They'd pick me out a mile away, and my accent would be my downfall. How are you?"

"Happier because you are here."

"Where can we talk?"

"We will go to my bungalow," said Phiroshah. "I have told my chauffeur to take Mrs. Mannering there when she has finished her drive."

They walked towards another Daimler. As they drove through the city, Mannering felt the fascination of the hordes of people, the thronging roads, the reckless traffic, the careless gharry-drivers. Horns blared incessantly. Policemen gave vigorous signals which some motorists actually obeyed. Phiroshah sat back, smiling, untroubled, while Mannering looked about him.

They turned into the Marine Drive. The tide was out, rocks showed above the surface of the water. Hotels and tall houses ringed the bay. A few people walked along the wide promenade. There was little traffic here, and for some distance it was a dual carriageway. They turned left with the drive, then uphill, then sharply to the right up a steep hill. Large houses were on either side, most of them hidden by trees. They turned into a gateway, and a big, old-fashioned house, with ornate carving and narrow windows, stood at the end of the drive.

Mannering had pictured a single-storey building; this "bungalow" was at least three storeys high.

White-clad boys were at the door.

Phiroshah led Mannering across a spacious, barely furnished hall towards double-doors which stood wide open. These led into a long, narrow room. The floor was polished, and there were some skin rugs. Silken cushions were on the floor, but there were also couches and easy chairs. Heavy silken draperies hung from the wide window overlooking the harbour, and from the doors.

They rustled at one door as if in the wind.

The double-doors through which they had come were closed. The boys stayed outside. Phiroshah led the way to chairs in front of the window. The view was magnificent; the water of the bay had the pure blue of the sky.

"Now we can talk freely," Phiroshah said. "I can see that you are worried, and—"

Mannering said: "Not very worried, yet, but I think I'm going to be." He glanced at the doorway where the curtains had rustled. They were still, but something behind them prevented them from hanging straight. He took a step forward.

The curtains were convulsed as if by a high wind. A small, dark figure, naked except for a loin cloth, darted out. The knife in his hand was curved, cruel. Mannering shot out a foot, the man leapt over it and hurled himself towards Phiroshah with the knife raised.

Mannering's hand was in his pocket, fingers about a gun.

He fired through his pocket. The naked man coughed and

sprawled forward. The knife slipped out of his hand and fell at Phiroshah's feet.

CHAPTER TEN

THE STORY

MANNERING heard the doors opening behind him, and the rush of feet. Before he could reach his victim, two servants were standing over the man. Phiroshah spoke gently, without any sign of flurry. They lifted the naked man, one taking the shoulders and the other the legs, and carried him out.

Blood dripped on the polished floor from the wound; a servant wiped it up.

The doors closed.

Phiroshah said: "I was in your debt when you agreed to come and help me, Mannering. Now I owe you my life."

Mannering didn't speak.

"Did you see him?" asked the old man.

"I saw the curtains bulge."

"I am getting too old," said Phiroshah. "And one of my servants is disloyal, or the man could not have found a way in. Please sit down." Mannering sat down in an easy chair overlooking the bay, taking his hand out of his pocket; there was a small bullet hole, which had frayed the cloth. "If he lives, they will try to make him talk, but it will not be easy. Probably he was just ordered to come here and kill me. If necessary, I will see him myself."

"The police might even be interested."

Phiroshah smiled. He had good teeth and they looked natural.

"They will deal with him later. They are my good friends, Mannering, although they know nothing of the blue diamonds.

There is a question burning in your mind. What is it?"

They could talk about the attack later.

Mannering said: "Why send for me? I don't know the criminals here, the ways of the criminals, the law—anything. I can only work blindly."

"As you have this morning!"

"That was luck."

"Haven't I heard you called Lucky John Mannering? You may know something of this already. You are not a man to act blindly. I know your love of jewels and your skill in probing for the truth. I am in great personal difficulty, because of my grievous losses and—uncertainty. You read of the Rangipore jewels, of course."

"Yes."

"Then you know that it is said that a group of fanatical patriots who do not think our Government's attitude towards certain princes is strong enough have appointed themselves judges and executors. They have stolen – taken – jewels from many of our princes who live much of the time out of India. They *say* that these jewels will be sold to alleviate distress in the famine states, but there is no evidence of this yet. I doubt their honesty of purpose. They could be murderous thieves. The police have had no success against them. You understand?"

"Yes."

"Now I, who have suffered so much, begin to wonder if these men have some leader whom no one suspects, who has a form of protection – such as a high position in government. That is one aspect. The other is this. The Maharajah of Ganpore has a very fine collection of jewels including the blue diamonds. He wishes to sell them, and is nervous about the fanatics. Already the murder of my sons suggests that the group is after the blue diamonds. Now! I have suggested to the Maharajah that you could dispose of them for him, and could help to outwit and uncover the fanatics – find out the truth. I tell you, Mannering, I am not sure that anyone here *wants* to know the truth."

Mannering said evenly: "Let me get this straight. I am to act as agent for the Maharajah of Ganpore, taking the risk of a head-on clash with the fanatics who use dacoit methods. I'm to smuggle, or find a way of smuggling—"

"No, it is not a question of smuggling. There is no law to prevent the Maharajah sending or taking all his jewels out of the country. The fanatics – shall we give them a name? the Bundi, as they are known – make the danger."

"Why Bundi?"

"After their leader, it is said. A figurehead – a man who was prominent in anti-British political circles years ago and transferred his hatred to the pro-British princes. He is dead."

"Bundi is dead, long live the Bundi! And the Bundi is after the Maharajah of Ganpore." Mannering watched the saintly face and wondered what went on behind the friendly brown eyes. "Tell me more about the Maharajah."

"He is extremely wealthy – and has fifty of the blue diamonds."

Mannering drew in his breath.

"You are astounded, of course. Yes, in all there are fifty-one. They are set in jewellery which has no equal in India – in brooches, pendants, ear-rings, tiaras, bracelets, necklets. They were collected centuries ago by the first Maharajah of Ganpore for his wife, and they were buried with her in a tomb which is second, I think, only to the Taj Mahal." Phiroshah stood up, went across to a cabinet and with great deliberation poured out a whisky and brought it to Mannering on a tray, with water and soda.

"There is still prohibition in Bombay; it is better not to have the servants see this. Now, please follow me carefully. A year ago, the tomb of the first Ranee was broken open. Such an abominable sacrilege! There is untold wealth in the tombs in India, but pillage such as this has seldom been known. The Bundi was named – quietly, in whispers. The Maharajah recovered the jewels. He foresaw a future in which there would be great changes, reasoned that one day even the sanctity of tombs would be ravaged by the Government. More – he saw the evil of famine and poverty existing by the side of entombed and wasted wealth. He decided – so he has told me – to sell them and use the proceeds to help the people of his own state."

Phiroshah paused again. Mannering sipped his whisky and studied the old man's face. Phiroshah seemed to feel the story deeply.

"The Maharajah called for me, because I have sold many of his jewels to America, a few elsewhere. They must be taken overseas to get the most for them. Understand, the Maharajah does not like the new form of government and the loss of autonomy of the states, but he has been loyal. Ganpore is a small state, not easily accessible, and is run well. Among other things, he installed a system of dams and irrigation; there is no famine. He is respected by the Government. No man should be so safe from the Bundi. The attempts on his jewels make me doubt the motives of the Bundi. Of course, I am hated by them. I serve the princes."

Mannering studied the profile against the brightness of the sky, and wondered.

"Now please, your questions," Phiroshah said gently.

Mannering leaned back, very thoughtfully.

"Other things first. The Bundi is after the blue diamonds, knows your part in it, killed your sons, followed your daughter, raided my shop. They're strong, they're ruthless. You'd suffered so much already. Why risk Shani?"

Phiroshah sat very still.

"Well, why?" Mannering's voice was harsh.

"She was well-guarded," Phiroshah said. "She is like a son. I am too old, and I could trust no one else with the story. Her guards had to protect her; they know nothing about the blue diamond."

"Are you sure?"

"Yes, Mannering."

"You trust Shani?"

"With my life."

"She saw a man connected with those who raided my shop afterwards. A man named Banu. So did my bearer, Amu."

Phiroshah smiled faintly. Admiringly? "You are a remarkable man. Yes, she did. Banu is not one of my servants, but is an acquaintance. Amu told me that Banu worked against you. Shani saw him, to lull any suspicions he might have of her knowledge. Amu cabled me the information, but if Banu has returned to India, it is secretly; I have not been able to trace him. He could well be with the Bundi. He was prominent in anti-British societies. But Banu is insignificant. You might get at the truth through him, but there are others, more important men."

Mannering said: "I don't get it, Phiroshah. The police—"

"The police have tried. I do not believe they tolerate the Bundi, although certain highly placed people do. But the Bundi has adherents everywhere. The Maharajah has become desperately anxious to sell, to be free from trouble. I recommended you. When you did not answer his letters, he tried elsewhere. Several dealers from America and Europe are at or on their way to Ganpore now. I was not satisfied, so—I sent Shani and the diamond. Now—"

Mannering said: "So there is competition."

"If you can call it that." Phiroshah smiled. "Knowing they were coming made me more anxious to have you here. I decided that I would succeed where the Maharajah had failed. You say that I judged you by your newspaper reputation." The smile was one of mild amusement. "Not that alone, my friend. I had met you, I had seen you work. I could well imagine that you would not be prepared to come to India simply to bid against other dealers—but there was a way to bring you here. I promised the Maharajah that I would succeed where he had failed, and—"

Mannering said: "The Maharajah didn't approach me."

"My friend, he wrote to you!"

"I didn't get a letter."

"You can be sure he wrote. I was puzzled when you didn't answer." Phiroshah paused, then went on softly: "The letter was intercepted, then, by someone who wanted to prevent you from coming."

"Who knew that he had written to me?" Mannering asked.

CHAPTER ELEVEN

MANNERING PLANS

PHIROSHAH walked towards the window and looked out. Excitement glowed in his eyes, the excitement of hope. It was a long time before he answered and then he seemed to speak to himself.

"His son and his secretary knew."

"A European?"

"No. An Indian."

"No one else."

"No one who should have known," said Phiroshah. "Is it possible, Mannering? That the letter was never sent?"

"Probable."

"You will admit that I was right in wanting you here."

Mannering smiled. "I'm not complaining, although I've been given plenty of notice that I'm not wanted. I had 'Don't go' notes in London and on the aeroplane, and 'Go back' notes when I reached here."

Phiroshah asked softly: "How frightened they are of you!"

"Or how careful." Mannering lit another cigarette. "Do you know a bookseller named Patandi?"

"I know of him, yes. He is a rogue."

"He had my brief-case," said Mannering, and explained. Phiroshah listened without expression, but anger soon sparked in his eyes.

"You handled that situation well. Patandi is a rogue, and can be bought by anyone's money. We must try to find out who paid him for this. He is a coward, also, and might yield under pressure."

"Not yet," said Mannering. "And if he'll take anyone's money, he'll take mine."

"Mine," corrected Phiroshah. "Now, Mannering, what do you think of this? Are you glad you came?"

"I'm warming up," said Mannering. He looked quite detached as he finished his whisky and soda. "So there's a house party at the palace, with some dealers on the way, and me to follow. Who are the others?"

"Petter and Kyneton of New York, Duval of Paris and van Groot of Amsterdam."

"Not a bad assortment," Mannering said. "When is the auction to start?"

"Three days from now. Two of them are going by train, and that takes two full days. The others are flying—may already be there, in fact. You will fly?"

"I'll think about it," Mannering said. "Someone is so anxious to keep me away that it might be an idea to let the world think I'm not going."

Nothing stirred outside; there was only the beauty of the sun on the water. The tide was coming in and all but the higher rocks were covered.

"I could go as a bearer or a servant—with you," said Mannering. "There are tall Hindus. Patandi, for instance. The snag will be the language, so the big bearer will have to be dumb. Make-up shouldn't be difficult. I'm fairly well-tanned, and with some careful work I can have the right complexion. A turban and a dhoti – although I'm not sure that I could manage a dhoti. It would show too much leg, anyhow." His eyes were half closed and he spoke dreamily. "Sikhs are big chaps usually, aren't they? A lot of them wear long breeches, too. Hot, but I can stand that. I can fix a beard, too – their religion forbids them to cut their hair, doesn't it? Yes, a Sikh. The question would be whether to tell the Maharajah. Let's think about it – whether I'm to go as myself or in disguise." Phiroshah was smiling. "What will your wife say?"

"Go as myself, or she can't go," said Mannering promptly. "We'll see."

Phiroshah said: "You are a most remarkable man, with an equally remarkable wife."

Ten minutes later Lorna was ushered in. She looked flushed with the heat, but there was rapture in her eyes. She squeezed Phiroshah's hands in greeting. "Thank you for bringing me."

"I hope you will always feel like that," said the old man. "Now, we shall have lunch."

They left Phiroshah's bungalow a little after three. Lorna wilted in the heat, and Mannering went back with her to the hotel. She took a shower and rested, with a magazine. Mannering dressed again after his shower in a suit of cream linen.

Lorna looked at him from the bed. "Fantastic's the word for you," she said. "Don't you feel the heat?"

"It's tolerable."

"Where are you going?"

"I thought a chat with Mr. Patandi wouldn't be a bad idea."

Lorna knew everything – except about the attack on Phiroshah. The old man had not broached the subject again. Lorna said: "Be careful."

"We've that week's grace, remember."

She stretched out an arm to make the electric fan go faster. It stirred her hair without really making her cool.

"Don't take too much for granted," she said.

Mannering laughed, and went out, spoke to Amu, and walked downstairs with Joseph. The sun was glaring down, but not far off was a bank of heavy cloud. Everyone, even beggars, stood about listlessly in what shade they could find. A party of tourists stopped outside the Gateway and looked as if they couldn't have cared less had they been in hell. It burned like that. In a little patch of shade not far along three venerable gharry drivers were standing by their gharries; the horses drooped.

"We'll take one of those," Mannering said.

"Yes, sahib." Joseph went quickly to the nearest gharry and Mannering studied the people lounging near. One looked very much like another. He tried to photograph them on his memory as he climbed into the gharry. Joseph sat beside the squatting driver.

No one hurried, but the city streets were crowded. Shopkeepers kept inside their little shops. Through the doorways of the larger shops and offices people were waiting in the comparative coolness, glad to be out of the sun. Only a few Europeans were about, the women carrying parasols.

They turned off a wide street into a narrow one with a cobbled roadway. Cars were parked on one side, and heat radiated from them. White-clad Hindus moved slowly, sluggishly across the road. They turned into a still narrower street, where there was hardly room for two cars to pass. The clip-clop of the horse's hooves made almost the only sound. Native shops were on either side – tiny places, no more than holes in the wall, filled with merchandise. A carpenter sat outside a shop sawing, the only sign of activity.

The sun was blotted out, but the heat seemed worse. Mannering's body was damp from head to foot.

The gharry stopped as a few drops of heavy rain fell. Immediately alongside was a tiny shop with the name *I. Patandi* above it. Books were crammed in one window, mostly second-hand and poor-looking volumes. Leather goods and carvings, all cheap souvenirs, filled the other window. Mannering climbed down from the gharry as the rain belched out of the skies; his coat was damp before he reached the shop. Joseph paid off the driver and waited in a nearby alley.

There was room for a single counter in the middle of the shop, crammed with books and nicknacks, and for three people to move; that was all. The shelves were filled with junk from floor to ceiling.

A little old man in European clothes came up from a corner.

"Mr. Patandi is expecting me," Mannering said. "My name is Mannering."

"Yes, sahib," the little man said, and disappeared into the back of the shop through a tiny doorway. There was whispering and scuffling; then a boy of nine or ten came out, darted past Mannering and raced off into the rain. It was so hot that Mannering went to the door. Water splashed up at him, but at least it gave an illusion of coolness. Several Indians were taking what shelter they could. He didn't see one he recognised, except Joseph, who was in the dry.

The little old man was near.

"Beautiful books, sahib; very beautiful books. Very beautiful."

"No thanks," said Mannering.

The soft, pleading voice went on and on. "Books, souvenirs, hand-beaten copper, Kashmir inlay." Mannering didn't answer again, just stared at the teeming rain. Was he being watched, or just noticed? He waited for seven or eight minutes, until the boy turned the corner, splashing through water which was now several inches deep in the steep gutters. Immediately behind him came an unbelievable figure – Patandi, carrying an umbrella.

Patandi stepped through puddles with fastidious care, holding the black umbrella high above his head; it made him look a giant. He glanced up, saw Mannering and waved joyously – and stepped into a puddle, which splashed up to his knees. He laughed until his whole body shook, and the laughter seemed to waft him to the doorstep. Mannering stepped inside and Patandi squeezed through.

He beamed.

"The wise Englishman, how quickly you come! I congratulate you. The rain is just a little storm; it will soon pass and we shall start, yes? With the famous lady? Or . . ." His aniseed-breath swept over Mannering, and he gave an obscene wink, "we start alone, sir? Just you and me? Oh, the things I can show you, the—"

"We start by sending everyone but you and me out of the shop," said Mannering. "Out of the back of the shop, too."

Patandi's eyes widened. He looked puzzled, and he hesitated. Mannering went to the back of the shop and bent down to look through the tiny doorway.

"No!" cried Patandi, and hurled himself at Mannering and dragged him away.

CHAPTER TWELVE

MONEY TALKS

MANNERING allowed himself to be dragged from the door, then gripped Patandi's wrist, twisted, and sent him thumping against one of the walls. Books fell in a shower on his head. Patandi gasped with pain. His face was distorted. Mannering did not doubt that it was naked fear. There was no malevolence – just fear. Patandi licked his lips.

"I beg the sahib's pardon. I did not mean to touch him. You understand – my wife." He pointed to the door.

Mannering said: "Either she leaves, Patandi, or I go to the police."

Patandi's face turned a greenish-white. Mannering watched as he went towards the door, poked his head through, and then wriggled; it seemed impossible for him to get his great bulk through there, but he disappeared. There was more furtive whispering.

A woman appeared, holding her sari in front of her face, and ran out through the street-door. Another. A third, who looked little more than a girl. Two others followed, also girls. Next, a boy. Mannering hadn't seen more than the dark hole beyond and smelt the fetid air; he had not dreamed that so many people were crowded in there.

Patandi called out, and the little old man in European clothes went sadly off into the rain. This beat down noisily against the front of the shop and into the street.

Patandi wriggled through again, and even managed a mockery of a smile.

"All gone, Mr. Mannering, all gone."

"I'd like to be sure."

Patandi waved to the door. "See, mister!"

Mannering bent down and poked his head through. It was gloomy in there, and the stench was revolting. A small window, high up in the wall, gave the only light. He could see well enough to be sure that no one else was present. He coughed, backed to the door and took in deep gulps of fresh air, then turned back to Patandi. Mannering moved the counter across the opening into the rear room. No one could hear through that.

"I wait, mister," said Patandi.

"Who stole my brief-case? The boy who just ran out?"

"Mister, he is my son. I try to make him a good boy, as good as a Christian, but no, mister, he lies, cheats, steals. I beat him, I—"

"You sent him to the airport, told him who to look for, told him what to do."

Patandi's hands were intertwining.

"Mister—"

"Why did you do it? Who did you do it for?"

Patandi looked as if he would soon be in tears.

"I am sorry, mister. That boy is a great worry, I cannot make him honest; I—"

"You've taught him to be a cheat, but I'm not here about that. Who gave you the orders to get my case? Who did you take it to? Who sent you back with it, and with that story of a week in Bombay?"

Patandi's voice was shrill.

"Mister, mister, it is not true! I swear by the sacred serpent, it is not true."

Mannering said: "How much were you paid?"

Patandi stopped moistening his lips and protesting, and looked owlish.

"How much?" Mannering insisted.

"Mister—I am a poor man, and you are a wise one. You see in the darkness. I have to keep my wives, my family, so many children." Patandi spread his arms round, as if to imply that he had as many children as books. He spat the last words. "Two hundred rupees!"

"It wasn't more than fifty."

"Mister! One hundred and fifty rupees—"

Mannering took out his case, selected some notes; Phiroshah had changed cheques for him. He counted out two hundred rupees in twenty-rupee notes, held them loosely, put his wallet away, and said: "Who was it?"

"You will not betray me, mister?"

"I want to know who you worked for. If you tell me the truth, I won't name you or go to the police. If you lie, I'll tell the police what I saw in there."

Patandi gulped.

"I am a poor man, mister; an honest man." He darted a greedy look at the two hundred rupees. "I tell only the truth. I live to serve the wise Englishman." He gulped again and muttered: "It was the wretched man, Patel, Imannati Patel; you will find him in the telephone directory. Please, mister."

He moved across the room. The telephone, of the candlestick type, stood in a recess, with the directory hanging from by a cord. He thumbed it over. Mannering watched the grimy forefinger go down the list of Patels. There were dozens of them – hundreds.

The finger stopped, pointing.

Mannering read: "Imannati Patel, 81 Woodham Road." He wrote it in a small notebook, added the telephone number, and drew back. Patandi licked his lips as he looked at the money. Mannering handed it over and looked towards the little door.

"I hope this is true."

"I would not lie to you, mister. Patel himself told me. I was to bring you the brief-case, I was to frighten you. I said to myself the moment that I saw you, this man will not be frightened. Patel, he is a fool." Patandi was counting the money and his fingers shook. "A thousand thanks, mister. Thank you very much."

Mannering went out.

He stopped at the threshold, startled; water was still rushing down the gutters, but the rain had stopped and the sky was clear overhead. It was cooler, too. More people were walking about, the shopkeepers no longer looked so sleepy. Two beggars approached, but Joseph pushed them aside.

"Where now, sahib?"

"We'll walk a little way," said Mannering. "You follow, Joseph. I want to know if anyone follows me."

"Yes, sahib."

"Were we followed from the hotel?"

Joseph considered, then smiled; his teeth showed very white against his dark skin.

"No, sahib."

"Make sure, now."

Mannering walked towards the corner, trying to remember the way the gharry had come. The streets looked narrow but cleaner. Shops on one side of the next street had been boarded up, but the boards were being taken down; on the other side they had been protected against the rain. Children splashed through muddy-looking puddles. Mannering kicked up mud as far as his knees and slackened his pace. He took three more turnings and then saw a wide main street ahead, with cars moving in each direction. He headed for this and waited at the corner. As he looked round, he tried to see whether anyone but Joseph had followed him. He recognised no one, but wasn't sure; in London he would have been.

Lorna was still lying on the bed, the magazine on the floor; a tea tray was on the bedside table, with two cups. She wore a negligée of some flimsy material.

"Have a cup, darling? It's much cooler after the rain, and I just had to have a drink."

"Two cups, please," said Mannering.

She poured out. "Did you have to walk? You've ruined that suit."

"It'll clean up," said Mannering. "Patandi has given me the name of the man who paid him to work his trick. Patandi has about a dozen wives, and they all live in a room a quarter – an eighth the size of this." He drank his tea, and leaned across and lifted the telephone.

Phiroshah's number was on a pad near the telephone.

"So soon, my friend?"

"Is it wise to talk over the telephone?" asked Mannering.

"No. I will come and see you."

"Thank you," said Mannering. He rang off, and Lorna was looking at him through her lashes. He saw the drawing-pad by the side of the bed for the first time, picked it up, and was startled. Lorna's drawing was always good, but he'd seen nothing better than this. Patandi, Phiroshah, Amu, Joseph – all of them looked up at him from the pad. There were a dozen pencilled drawings, firm, vivid types he recognised from his brief encounters.

"Sure you wouldn't like to stay here while I go diamond hunting?"

"No," she said. "I can finish these any time. It's odd, but the only one I would like to sit for me is Patandi. Do you think—"

"He'll do anything we ask, he's so scared."

"Of whom?"

"You'll find out," said Mannering. He went into the dressing-room. All his clothes had been pressed and were in the wardrobe. He had another shower and changed leisurely; it was now pleasantly cool. By the time he had finished, there was a tap at the door. He went into the sitting-room, where Phiroshah was waiting.

"So you saw Patandi," said Phiroshah promptly.

"Did Joseph tell you?"

"Yes. I'm not sure that you should do that kind of thing yourself. These men can be dangerous, and you have much more important things to do."

Mannering said mildly: "Could they be more important than getting the name of Imannati Patel?"

Phiroshah said very softly: "I*mannati* Patel?"

"Of course, the bookseller could have lied."

"Yes," said Phiroshah, "but I doubt if he would have named the man unless it were true. How did you do it?"

"He had a guilty secret in his back room," said Mannering. "I don't know what it was, but made him think that I did. So Imannati's a known bad man."

"Imannati Patel is as evil a man as I know in Bombay," said Phiroshah with quiet vehemence. "Evil and dangerous. I did not know that he was interested in jewels. In drugs, yes. Not jewels.

Always in drugs." He frowned as he walked slowly about the room. "So – if the Bundi used such a man, the Bundi is no group of high-minded patriots."

"Can he be frightened?" asked Mannering.

"No. You cannot deal with Patel as you did with the bookseller. Don't attempt to tackle Patel yourself."

Mannering sat down.

"I'm at a disadvantage because I don't know how the methods work over here, and don't really know the temperament, but that's a double-edged sword," Mannering said. "Or it could be. They aren't familiar with my methods and the direct approach could disconcert them. Think about it. I'd say that I ought to see Patel soon."

Phiroshah said: "I am afraid that you will, however I advise you."

"If I go openly, and have Amu and Joseph waiting for me outside, what can go wrong?"

"It is not the immediate danger but the danger that lies in wait. Against men like Patel – forgive me – you are as a nymph to a serpent. Let us be very cautious."

He broke off.

There was a sound outside. Amu's voice was raised, then a woman's. The wailing grew louder, laden with anguish. Amu spoke roughly, but couldn't stop it. Phiroshah stepped towards the door, opened it an inch, and looked out. Mannering was able to see over his head.

A woman was on her knees in front of Amu, hands stretched out in supplication. The wailing ceased; she talked in a low-pitched voice.

Amu stepped away from her, stern-faced, but unable to stop the flow. Phiroshah drew back into the room and closed the door. The wailing started afresh.

Mannering said: "What did she say?"

"My friend, she said that I am right and that you would be foolish to go to Patel, to let Patel know that Patandi talked to you. She is Patandi's wife, his favourite wife. She is mourning him, and more than that – she has been persuaded to come and see you, bringing a grimmer warning than Patandi's."

Mannering echoed: "*Mourning* him."

"She told Amu that the bookseller was killed soon after you left the shop," said Phiroshah. "His throat was cut."

CHAPTER THIRTEEN

MR. IMANNATI PATEL

LORNA was at the balcony window, books propped up to make a drawing-board, pencil busy. Mannering stood by the door, watching her complete absorption. Pencil and brush, paper and canvas, were to her what jewels were to him. He would risk his neck for jewels; their lure made danger fade, dulled his mind alike to risk and to the affairs of daily life. The beauty of the stones was a magnet and he could never wholly resist it.

Lorna couldn't resist the spell of India. It brought to her art new virile life; obsessing her.

She finished a sketch and leaned back, stared down at the pencilled lines, actually smiled. Mannering tiptoed across the carpeted floor and kissed the nape of her neck.

She started. "John!"

"Dream-world," said Mannering. "Go back; my sweet, you look at your loveliest in it."

"I've finished." She looked at the sketch critically, yet not dissatisfied. Mannering, hands on her shoulders, peered at it. His heart contracted, for the dead Patandi looked up at him in black and white. Patandi with his great wondering eyes which yet held a hint of cruelty; with his little rosebud of a mouth, his fat cheeks, his buried chin. Lorna lifted the sheet; beneath it was another Patandi, smiling with all the childish intensity of the world, eager, aggressive; and the hint of cruelty also showed there. Another sheet, and Patandi appeared with narrowed eyes, chin thrust forward, threat in his expression – the earnest Patandi who had tried to frighten them.

Lorna put the sheets on top of one another and shook them into position.

"Do you really think he'll sit for me?"

Mannering pressed her shoulders gently.

"Not now," he said.

He felt her stiffen. She turned her head sharply. She read the truth, and shivered as she stood up.

"What happened?"

"He was killed."

"Oh, God!" Lorna said, and torment tore at her voice. "Why did that have to happen? Why did it have to happen now? Why couldn't we have a few days of calm?" She looked at the sketch of the dead man on top of the others. "We shouldn't have come. I oughtn't to have made you. There's evil here. Beneath the beauty and the colour and the heat there's cruelty. It wraps itself round one, it touches everybody. We must go back."

Mannering said: "It's not all so cruel."

He had seen her in these moods before, without quite understanding them. Now, shock had quenched her blazing enthusiasm, and she was stricken. She had barely touched the pulse of the city, but she knew the symptoms and had seen beneath the surface. There was the cruelty of indifference to human suffering, and she was too sensitive to remain unaware of it for long. Probably she had consciously accepted it but fought it back, excited by the opportunities which the beauty gave her.

"We must go back, John." She spoke more normally. "It's my fault that we came. You didn't really want to. I told myself that you were fooling, but I can see it now. You weren't certain of yourself, weren't certain that it was the right place. It isn't."

"Once Phiroshah's problems are over, it'll be smooth sailing," Mannering said, "and you'll see the good with the bad. The Maharajah, for instance, and his good work in Ganpore." He smiled and held her shoulders firmly. "We've a lot to do. Patandi named a man I'm going to see right away. Afterwards, we may have to leave quickly. Probably I'll have to do the disappearing trick."

She didn't speak.

"And rely on Phiroshah," Mannering said.

Phiroshah was squatting on a low, tapestry-covered stool, legs crossed beneath him. He looked troubled. Mannering found himself lighting a cigarette and avoiding the old man's eyes.

"I'm going to see Patel," he announced.

Phiroshah nodded.

"I'd like Amu to stay here and look after my wife. Can you let me have another man to come with me and Joseph?"

"Yes, my friend."

"Or rather, come after me," said Mannering. "I'll go ahead, with Joseph, and the other man will follow, to make sure whether I'm followed. I can't tell one man from another – they look so much alike."

"You'll learn to distinguish them."

"I hope so. What happened to that man I shot?"

Phiroshah didn't answer.

Mannering said jerkily: "If I can't be sure that you're going to tell me everything, I might as well give up. Why did he try to kill you? Where did he go? Have the police been told? Has he talked?"

"He died without talking," said Phiroshah.

Mannering felt as if sharp claws had jagged into him.

"I interrogated each one of my servants closely, and the man who had let him in confessed. He was bribed to allow the assailant in. He swears that he did not think there would be an attempt to kill me. He also named the man who bribed him. Not everyone would know, but I can tell you that the man who bribed him is in Patel's employ."

Mannering said: "Another good reason for seeing Patel."

"A better one for keeping away from him," said Phiroshah. "My friend, you have to prepare against deadly methods and great cunning. I have told the police what happened at my house but did not say that you shot the man. I said that he attacked me and I shot him myself. There will be no unpleasantness. The man was a hired thug; they're glad he's dead. But there may be others who will talk to Patel. They may tell Patel that you killed the man. Patel could use that against you. Mannering, I think you should keep away from Patel. The quicker you leave Bombay for Ganpore—" He broke off, slid off the stool and walked close to Mannering, and the dignity of his bearing made Mannering forget his small stature. "Of course I shall understand it if you prefer to return to England."

Mannering said woodenly: "Is anyone reliable?"

"Many, but – there is always the weak link in the chain."

"Can you find a man who will help me with my make-up? Get me the clothes, show me how to work quick changes? If it isn't a man who can be relied on not to talk I'll manage myself."

"I can find the man you want," Phiroshah said. "Do you want him now?"

"Tonight," said Mannering, "and again tomorrow, so that we can work in daylight as well as artificial. I'd better go to him."

"I will arrange it," said Phiroshah. "And Patel?"

Mannering lit another cigarette, relaxed, looked as if he hadn't a worry in the world.

"I'll go to him right away," he said.

Woodham Road was not far from the bustling heart of the city, a backwater where few people walked, few cars passed. There was ample parking space on either side of the road. As Mannering walked along the street, with Joseph just behind him, he seemed to be in a European city. The houses, standing back from the road, were more European than Indian; only the palm trees and unfamiliar shrubs in some of the gardens made it different. He reached No. 81, walked past and crossed the road, then passed again on the other side. The house was old and looked dilapidated. The drive was untidy, the paintwork needed another coat.

Phiroshah's other bearer walked past on the far side of the road as Mannering approached No. 81. The man would have spoken to Joseph had they been followed. Joseph waited outside, and Mannering walked up the drive. The main door was at the side. Bougainvillaea grew wild over the wall; the gravel of the path was muddy and untended. The brass bell and knocker needed cleaning.

Mannering pulled the bell, heard it clanging, stood listening. After a long time, soft footsteps sounded on the other side of the door.

A servant dressed in grubby-looking white clothes, long coat and baggy trousers opened the door a few inches and peered out. His dark eyes seemed nervous.

"Sahib?" he whispered.

Mannering put his foot against the door.

"I want to see the master, Imannati Patel," Mannering said.

"Sahib?" The eyes looked blank.

"Mr. Patel," said Mannering. "I must see him. Take me to him."

"Please," said the boy. He opened the door a little more, and Mannering stepped through. The hall was narrow and dark. Old furniture, thick with dust, lined the walls in no sort of order. A big glass showcase stood in one corner, empty apart from baize-lined shelves. The windows were of coloured glass, keeping out the light. A staircase ran from the hall, a narrow passage alongside it.

"Please," repeated the boy.

He turned and walked up the stairs, glancing back to make sure that Mannering followed him. The first landing was dark and shadowy. There were pieces of tall furniture, large enough to hide a man; easily large enough to hide a small man such as Phiroshah's attacker. Apart from the padding sound of the boy's footsteps, there was no sound. Mannering felt the eeriness.

A door stood open, showing a large room furnished like a Paris salon. The furniture looked so old and neglected that it might really be Louis Quinze; everything was faded and seemed dirty. The Venetian blinds were drawn down at all the windows, allowing only a little light through the wooden slats.

The boy padded on.

He stopped at an open door, bowed, and held his hands out, in invitation to Mannering. Mannering felt his fingers tighten instinctively about his gun as he stepped through.

This was a big, high-ceilinged room. Furniture was placed without order at the walls. In the middle was a large brass bedstead, with a bamboo table at one side. On the table were several bottles, one of white tablets, a cracked cup, a glass of pink liquid with a thermometer sticking out of it.

A man lay on the bed, with his back to this door.

Mannering saw the almost bald head through the bars of the bedstead. The sheet covering the man's body showed that he was big and tall. One big hand, brown and spotted and deeply veined, lay on the sheet. The boy didn't call out, did nothing to announce Mannering, just stood by the door. Mannering passed the head of the bed and looked down. The man on the bed had his eyes closed. The eyeballs were pressing against the veined lids, giving them an unnatural look. He had the curiously browny-pallid complexion of a Parsee. His face was lined, and the lines across his forehead were deep and dark. The bones stood out against the skin; it was a death's head of a face.

Mannering moved further away, stood by the head of the bed, looking down, watched by the boy, whose hands had disappeared into the sleeves of his coat.

The old man breathed softly.

Mannering saw two doors, as well as that through which he had come; both were ajar. He moved towards the nearest, holding his gun tightly. He opened it, and it squeaked. The room beyond was practically empty. A threadbare carpet covered the floor; there were small tables, two chairs and several cushions; and some old, seared prints on the wall – the glass in the frames of two of them was broken. Another open door was on the other side of the room. The bedroom could be approached from three directions. There was no way of watching all the doors at once. Mannering turned from this and walked past the foot of the bed to another opposite; it was also ajar. He pushed it wider – and backed away sharply, kicked against a table and sent a china ornament crashing to the floor. The noise of its breaking seemed like a gunshot.

In the other room, squatting, knees crossed, hands inside the sleeves of his jacket, was an old man, a very old man, turbanned, dressed in white. His black eyes were like ebony as he stared unblinkingly at Mannering.

The springs of the bed creaked.

"Who is it?" croaked the man on the bed. "Who is it?"

CHAPTER FOURTEEN

"GO BACK"

THE prominent eyes were open now and staring. The old man looked towards the side of the bed and his gaze moved slowly until he saw Mannering. He stopped moving his head, but didn't speak. The man in the next room sat unmoving. Mannering felt his fingers clammy round the steel of his gun. The old man's mouth moved; a big mouth, with almost shapeless lips. He bared yellow, wide-spaced teeth and spoke again in the croaking voice.

"Come here."

Mannering went a little nearer.

"Nearer." The invalid spoke in English. Would he speak in English if he didn't know who was present? "Here!" He raised his right hand and touched the side of the bed. His movements were slow and deliberate. Mannering had never felt himself so close to the presence of death.

He obeyed.

The other's eyes were light brown, seemed to be covered with a muddy film. He bared his teeth again.

"Who are you? What do you want?"

Mannering said: "I'm Mannering. John Mannering." He had been fooled. This wasn't Imannati Patel; it couldn't be.

The man on the bed said: "So Patandi told you."

Mannering felt as if he had been slashed by a whip. He shifted his position while the other eyed him with piercing appraisal. Now and again the man licked his lips. Then: "Sit down," he said.

An upright chair stood against the wall, just behind Mannering. He pulled it up and sat down. The other did not look away from him; seemed as if he were trying to read his thoughts. The silence dragged on.

"What do you want with me?" asked Patel abruptly.

Mannering said slowly: "I'm interested in murderers."

Seconds passed before Patel spoke again.

"Fool," he said. "Just a fool. I told you not to come. I could not have told you more plainly. Go back. Take your wife with you."

"I've a job to do," said Mannering.

"Not yours," said Patel hoarsely. "Nothing to do with you. Go back where you came from. Leave our affairs—to us. Don't be fooled by that old liar, Phiroshah. Only an idiot would listen to him."

It was bizarre enough in itself – the scene, the watching eyes, the sick man. The natural idiom in which Patel spoke, as if English were his mother tongue, heightened that, made everything more unreal. The flat statements, made as if there was no possible chance that he was wrong, spread doubts and uncertainty.

"I've a job to do," said Mannering. "I'll finish it."

"It will finish you," said Patel. "You *and* your wife. I told you what to do. Told Patandi to tell you. He did, didn't he?" Patel paused between each short sentence, as if talking and breathing both hurt him. "Have a week's holiday. See what you can. Go back. You won't run into trouble then. You'll be in trouble if—if you go to Ganpore. Only a fool would go to Ganpore; a bigger one would take his wife with him. Go back."

Mannering said: "Why do you want the blue diamonds?"

Patel didn't answer, just sneered.

"Who's paying you?" Mannering said.

Patel actually raised himself upon one elbow, pointed a bony finger, licked his lips, swallowed two or three times before he answered. There was froth at the corner of his lips.

"Damned insulting fool. Who is paying *me*? I don't accept anyone's money. I'm—I'm Imannati Patel. I work for no one. Don't let Phiroshah fool you. Always been enemies. We'll die enemies. He couldn't—beat me. I'm a sick man, very sick. Even now, Phiroshah can't beat me. Sent for you, to try. Old fool and young fool together. Go back."

He dropped on to his pillows, his breathing heavier. Mannering heard a rustle of movement. The old man from the corner room was moving forward. He reached the bedside table, opened the bottle of tablets, and put a tablet to Patel's mouth. Patel gulped it down. His breathing became hoarse, and the bed springs groaned under the convulsive movements of his body. The old man turned away and went back to the next room, leaving the door ajar.

Patel's eyes were closed; he looked as if he were falling into a drugged sleep. His breathing grew more steady; the bed stopped creaking.

Mannering got up, and the boy in the doorway turned and led the way downstairs. Still the only sound in the house was of his padding footsteps. He opened the front door and bowed low.

Mannering stepped into the street. It was still cooler, but anything would feel cool after the heat of that bedroom. He beckoned Joseph. The other bearer was walking up and down on the far side of the street, at least fifty yards away.

"We'll get a taxi," Mannering said.

"Yes, sahib."

There was a taxi a hundred yards along the road. Mannering sank back in his corner, wiped his forehead, lit another cigarette. He looked out of the window, and instead of seeing the walking people, saw the face of Imannati Patel – that death's head face. When he had bared his teeth, Patel had looked grotesque, obscene. Mannering turned to the other window; every man seemed to have the face of Patel.

He tapped on the window, and Joseph turned.

"To Mr. Phiroshah's house."

"Yes, sahib."

They drove to the Marine Parade and up the Malabar Hill, and the house already seemed familiar when it came in sight at the end of the long drive. The garden was immaculate; there could not be a greater contrast between this and Patel's. The taxi stopped. Mannering paid the driver, and walked up the steps. A servant opened the door, but Mannering didn't see the servant; he saw Shani.

It was the first time he had seen Phiroshah's daughter since he had arrived in India. She wore a sari of the familiar deep red, cloaking her as petals cloak a flower. She smiled with less gravity than he had known in London.

"I am very glad to see you, Mr. Mannering."

"Thank you, Shani."

"I have just been to see Mrs. Mannering," said Shani. "I will try to show her much of interest. Now, I have a message for you. My father has been called away, but he has arranged for the meeting tonight. Amu will know where to take you. The man whom you will visit is an expert in such make-up as you require."

"Will your father be long?"

"It is impossible to say." Shani raised her hands. "He did not expect to have to leave this evening. He hoped to see you again. He still hopes that he will be back before you retire." She smiled. "Can I offer you refreshment?"

"No, thanks." Mannering tried to put some enthusiasm into his voice. "You've been more than good. I'll go back to the hotel."

"I will tell the chauffeur," said Shani.

"I'd like to walk."

She raised her hands again, as if to say that she understood that an Englishman would walk when the rest of the world would ride. He went out. Shani stood at the top of the steps, smiling after him. Joseph followed. The other bearer was still in sight when Mannering reached the street itself. He walked briskly, in spite of the heat. The visit to Patel had been a sickening anti-climax; the visit to Phiroshah almost as bad.

Shani had been smooth – too smooth? Everything had been too smooth. He had relied on Phiroshah and no one else, and that was folly. Patel had called him a fool, and perhaps he was. He ought to get in touch with the English community; the European community, anyhow. They would know about Patel and Phiroshah, and they would give him a dispassionate opinion. He could make contact through the Embassy or through any of the clubs.

He reached the point in the road where it swept in a hair-pin turn to the left and the city, and led straight on past tall, shabby-looking houses. Beyond was a native quarter. He found himself sneering at the thought. It was all native; parts were built by Western standards, that was all. Did he have to remind himself that he was in India?

There was a traffic policeman in a crow's-nest, high above the corner, signalling to drivers who seemed to ignore him. Typical to place a policeman where he couldn't be seen. Mannering turned savagely round the corner. The road ran downhill. There were no buildings on either side at this spot; the houses were all up the hillside, above road level. There was a high wall on his left; the road on his right. He looked over the bay and the promenade, walking briskly. A few cars were coming from each direction; horns were blowing without the slightest need. Noise, dirt, squalor, misery – and mystery. He was already sick of it. He had been doubtful from the beginning, and . . .

He heard Joseph shout: "Sahib!"

He half turned. Joseph was twenty yards behind him, on the pavement. Two boys were kicking at him – just boys, ten or eleven years old, no more. Joseph didn't shout again, seemed to be covering his face with his arms. Mannering swung round.

Something clutched at his ankle and he went sprawling. As he fell, he saw a dark face peering at him from a hole in the wall on his left. He saw another. Hands stretched out, gripping him round the throat. He choked. He felt himself dragged head first into the hole. He hadn't a chance to shout, to struggle. The pressure at his throat grew stronger. He had to gasp for breath. His chest heaved.

The pressure relaxed.

He fell heavily, felt hands on him, felt a cloth being put over his head and drawn tightly round his neck. He struck out. Someone kicked him in the pit of the stomach; agony. He almost fell again, would have fallen but for the hands which clutched him. He felt himself being pushed along and pulled; hands seemed to be all round him. He felt cold – icy cold.

The pushing and the pulling stopped. He leaned against a wall. It seemed damp. The cloth over his face stopped him from seeing. He clawed at it, but felt a savage blow over the head as he touched the string. He staggered forward. A second blow pitched him into unconsciousness.

At least he was alive.

He lay on his back, on something hard. His head ached and his eyes ached, but he was alive. He could feel pain in his right shoulder, too – not severe, but uncomfortable. He moved little, because his feet were tied together. His hands weren't; that was odd.

He opened his eyes.

The bag had gone, but it was dark here. A faint light came from some way off – a flickering light of lamp or candle. He could hear nothing. He closed his eyes again, because the light was enough to hurt him. He moved his hands cautiously. It should be easy to draw up his legs and get at the cords round his ankles. No one could see what he was doing in this light.

He moved his legs slowly, but the cord was secured to the ground or the wall. He opened his eyes again, but could only see the dark shape of his body; couldn't make out the shape of the cords. He hitched himself forward, bending his knees all the time. Lying on his back, it was almost impossible to reach his ankles; not almost – it was impossible. He would have to turn over. He tried to turn towards the right, but the cord hampered him. He put out his hand again, made sure that the wall was on his right and turned slowly over on to his left side. Then he flattened himself against the wall and started to bend his knees again.

It was still difficult.

He strained his muscles, and the pain in his head grew worse. He stopped and relaxed. He would have to rest. The cords had been tied so that he couldn't get at them. If he stood up, then bent down, it should be easier; but getting to his feet would be an ordeal in itself.

He heard a sound close by.

He stiffened, and listened again. The sound was repeated —a little moaning sound. Someone else was here. He turned his head and tried to peer through the darkness, but he could see nothing. The groan came again, and almost immediately footsteps sounded. A man appeared, carrying an electric torch. It shone on Mannering's face and moved away. Mannering turned his head – and saw the light fall on Phiroshah's face.

CHAPTER FIFTEEN

PRISONERS

THERE was a dark patch on the side of the old man's face. Blood. As far as Mannering could see, it came from a wound in his forehead. His eyes were closed, and he didn't move although he moaned again.

Mannering looked towards the light. He could see the dark figure behind it, but nothing was clear.

The light shone on him again, and he blinked. Whoever carried the torch held it steady for a few seconds, then made the beam travel down to Mannering's legs. The cord showed; so did the foot or so of space between his ankles and the wall; one end was tied to a ring. The light went out.

The man turned and walked away, and soon there was no sound but Phiroshah's occasional groaning; no light but the glim a long way off.

Mannering lay back with his eyes closed and pictured the way the cord was fastened to the wall. The knot was on the right side, closest to the wall. The important thing to ease his position was to get it off the ring; that would be easier than getting it off his ankle. He lay close to the wall and, using his left hand, levered himself up to a sitting position; that was much easier than he had expected. He leaned forward and was able to touch the ring. His fingers moved about the cord until he touched the knot. He began to pick at it. The strain on his arm, shoulders and legs was too great to keep going long at a time.

He relaxed against the wall.

Belatedly, he felt in his pockets. Money was there – all the loose change; so were his keys. But his knife had gone, so had the gun. He rested again, then slid his left hand into his pocket; he had some English coppers and silver. He felt each piece, selected a thin coin, and drew it out. He ran his thumb round the smooth copper edge, then transferred it to his right hand and began to rub it against the stone floor.

He went on and on, making a little scraping sound, punctuated by groans from Phiroshah.

When he felt the coin again it was warm from the friction and there was an edge which felt quite sharp. He held the coin carefully and applied the new edge to the cord, sawing at it. The strain of holding the thin coin tightly made his arm stiff and sent pricking pains up to the elbow. He dared not let the coin go; he might never find it again in the darkness.

Suddenly his muscles twitched, his fingers lost their grip, the coin fell with a tinkling noise. A wave of anger and frustration made him feel sick. Suddenly, he jerked his feet away from the wall; nothing happened. He jerked again, savagely – and the cord broke.

He fell sideways, bumping his head.

He leaned against the wall for at least a minute, fighting against a sense of exultation. He bent down and worked on the knot round his ankles with both hands. It was not easy; the savage pull away from the wall had tightened the knot.

Phiroshah was silent.

Mannering felt the knot giving, pulled cautiously, and unfastened it. He stopped and listened; there was no sound. His ankles and feet tingled with the returning circulation. He rubbed them vigorously, and even the noise that he made worried him.

After a while, he got first to his knees and then to his feet. His ankles were almost too weak to hold him, and the right was worse than the left. He moved about gingerly. The pain eased until he felt that he could walk safely. He couldn't see how far it was to the opposite wall, and moved towards it, hands outstretched. He staggered three times before touching the broken surface with the palms of his hands.

He walked to and fro, making little sound, with the strength returning to his legs. His head ached, but it didn't stop him thinking. He hoped that it didn't affect his hearing. He heard faint sounds from some way off; another, nearer. Phiroshah had stirred. He turned and looked at the spot where the man was lying, and could just make out the shape of his body and the white clothes. He went to him and knelt down. He felt his pulse; it was very weak.

He took off his coat and spread it over the thin body, shivered, turned and went towards the light. He had been making up his mind to do that for a long time. Ten minutes, fifteen minutes; he didn't know. He guessed that he had been conscious for more than one hour and less than two.

The light was faint and yellow, and not direct. As he drew nearer, he saw a corner. He stepped to the side of the wall nearest the corner, listening intently but hearing nothing. He peered round.

In the room beyond – if room were the word for it, it was more a passage – four men were playing cards. They sat cross-legged. All were Hindus, dhoti-clad, with white turbans which were little more than twisted rags. One man's was rucked up near the waist; he wore a belt, and a naked knife was thrust through that, the blade flat against a skinny dark thigh.

The light from three wicks in little red earthenware crucibles cast flickering shadows, giving a touch of the sinister to a scene which was in itself peaceful. The light seemed to get better the longer Mannering stayed there.

None of the four card-players was facing him; none would be able to see him at casual glance. All were nearly black-skinned, with incipient beards and moustaches, and all looked clean apart from their clothes. An old box stood on one side, with four small round trays with little metal bowls on them – their food dishes. There was a chipped china jug. Close to the walls were bundles – their bedding.

He moved a little further out, increasing the risk of being seen, but he had to see everything within range. He saw his gun on the floor by the side of the box. The men were intent on their game; he could picture the size of each little pile of annas and rupees.

He felt in all his pockets; he had nothing which might serve as a weapon. If only he could get at his gun. He peered round the corner again, to measure the distance between him and the nearest man.

It was about six yards.

He could cover that in a running leap – two or three strides, at most. If he could get off to a good start he could scatter them and reach the gun. They would have time to recover and get their knives, but, once he had the gun, knives wouldn't matter.

The exit was beyond them, beyond that void. If he were to pull this off, he must prevent any one of them from escaping.

He went back behind the wall and bent up and down, flexing the muscles of his legs, testing his ankles. They were a little painful, especially the right one, but not enough to impede him. The task now was to get into a position for the attack without being seen. When he stepped right out into the passage he would be visible to two of the men if they glanced away from their cards.

He waited until they had finished dealing. They spoke in muted whispers, seeming to say what they wanted to say by nods and shaking of the head. Mannering stepped forward.

None of them looked up.

He stood poised for a second. They wouldn't know that he was on his way until he actually moved. If he could put two of them out of action at the first rush it would double his chances.

He leapt.

They heard him as his feet touched the floor after the first jump. He saw their heads jerk up and round, but he was on them before they moved. He flung out his right hand and smashed it into the face of the nearest man, paused long enough to kick a second and caught him on the side of the face. Both men went over. Another was on his feet, crouching, hand at his side, but he was too far away to strike with a single blow. Mannering reached the box and went down. He snatched the gun up, caught it firmly by the handle and swung round. A man was a yard away from him, knife upraised; the man slashed. Mannering felt his shirtsleeve rip.

He fired.

The shot roared out like a cannon, and the man pitched forward.

The other, knife in hand, hesitated just too long. Mannering shot the knife out of his hand. It fell, glinting in the light.

The others, recovered, stood with their knives ready. The first man he had wounded lay still on the floor.

Mannering said: "Drop your knives."

They didn't move, just stood crouching, wary, dangerous. Probably they didn't understand. He tried again.

"Drop your knives."

They didn't move.

Mannering fired at the knife of the nearest man, hit and shattered the blade. The other man dropped his as if it burned him. They straightened up, fearfully, and the third joined them. They were in a line in front of him. He said: "Turn round."

One spoke – in Hindi, or another language Mannering didn't understand.

Mannering raised his left hand, pointed downwards, and made a circular motion; they caught on quickly and spun round, facing a wall. He went forward, used his foot, kicked each man lightly behind the knees. They went down like puppets.

He had to go back to Phiroshah.

The three men lay with the uncanny stillness of Orientals, but Mannering could not be sure that they wouldn't jump up again.

He was wasting time.

He cracked each one behind the ear with the butt of his gun; they wouldn't spring up for a while. He stripped one man of his dhoti; there were yards of muslin in it, dirty and bedraggled. He tore it into strips, twisted one strip and bound the first man, used other strips for the remaining pair. He tore one strip into smaller pieces and stuffed them into the men's mouths.

Only the wounded man was free.

Mannering went across to him. He was unconscious, and the wound was high in the chest – too high, probably, for lung or heart. He tied the man's legs, loosely but in a way that would be difficult to undo, and did the same to his hands. Standing upright, the top of his head brushed the roof of the passage.

He went back towards the corner, stopped and picked up one of the lamps. The gentle light showed Phiroshah, still unconscious. Mannering lifted him gently and carried him to the other lights.

Phiroshah had a nasty knife wound in the temple and bruises on the back of his head, but he wasn't fatally injured – unless he were too old to stand the shock. Mannering wrapped his coat round him more closely, then lifted him again. He was able to pick up one of the crucibles in his left hand, and keep the gun in his right, with Phiroshah over his shoulder. He walked away from the now silent card-players, and seemed to walk for hundreds of yards. Then he saw the sky, the stars.

He laid Phiroshah down and crept forward; this was the entrance, and there would probably be a guard. He reached the gap at the end of the passage which was really a tunnel. He peered about him, but saw no shapes, nothing to suggest that anyone else was there. He ventured out a few paces. Nothing happened. He went back to the entrance, and peered out cautiously.

No one appeared.

Mannering went back for Phiroshah, lifted him and, with the old man over his shoulder, gun in hand and the light of the stars to guide him, stepped out of the tunnel. There were thick bushes and trees and, way above his head, the still, spectral heads of coconut palms. It was warm; not hot, but warm enough to bring the perspiration oozing out. He missed his footing once or twice, then came to a gap in the bushes.

He went through it.

As he saw a stretch of water, surface unruffled but peppered with the reflections of the stars, he also saw a man squatting at the water's edge.

CHAPTER SIXTEEN

THE LAKES

MANNERING lowered Phiroshah gently to the ground and straightened up. Apparently the squatting man had not heard him. He was twenty yards away, a dark figure, staring into the water. The stars were bright above their heads, and the water was like a gigantic mirror. Coconut palms fringed the edges of the lake, but the bush was thinner there. The ground was damp, but the mud was crumbly.

Mannering crept forward.

He was twenty feet from the man when the squatting figure stood up, without any sign of haste or alarm, and stared across the water. Mannering could have shot him; he kept the gun trained and stepped nearer.

The man turned.

He saw Mannering and gave a choking gasp, stepped back – and slipped. He fell backwards into the water. The splashes reached Mannering's waist. The surface was suddenly churned with fury; the stars danced on it. The man's figure showed clearly as he surfaced. The lake was deep – much deeper than Mannering had expected. The man hadn't a chance. All Mannering had to do was wait for him to scramble ashore.

Mannering waited.

He saw nothing new at first; heard a sudden rush through the water followed by a wild scream. Then he saw two great jaws open, heard them snap. The man screamed again, and disappeared. The water was beaten as by a sudden, lashing tumult, then gradually settled.

Horror choked Mannering. The scream, the snapping jaws, the swift disappearance – it hadn't been real. But it had happened – a crocodile had taken a victim.

The water must be infested, even so close to the land as this.

Mannering's mouth was dry and his lips felt cracked. He saw a long, narrow boat, little more than a canoe, tied up to a jetty made of long, straight logs lashed with ropes. The boat was still.

There was no way to the mainland, which looked so near, except by water.

He peered into the dark surface, imagining shapes which probably weren't there. He looked across at the mainland again, where the starry tops of the palms were dark and peaceful against the stars. They rose high above the other trees. He could see no light, nothing to suggest life.

He went to the jetty, walked along it, felt some of the logs give a little; and the water was very deep beneath it. He knelt down cautiously by the side of the boat. There was room for two, perhaps three, people. There were two paddles, with wide blades. At the bottom was a little water and an old tin.

If he waited here, others would come. He had little ammunition. His one real chance was to get to the mainland at once. He didn't know where he was; it might be hundreds of miles from Bombay – a day and a night might have passed since he had been kidnapped. He stood up cautiously, but the jetty seemed to rock.

Phiroshah hadn't moved.

Mannering lifted him and carried him to the jetty. In spite of the warmth, he felt cold. He lowered Phiroshah carefully into the canoe. It swayed up and down against the jetty. He stepped in gingerly, and the boat veered over, under his weight.

He stood upright, with the canoe swaying and water lapping over the side. He waited until it steadied. He could hear a sound now – the thumping of his heart. He lowered himself to the single seat, two logs lashed together, and picked up the paddles. Then he realised that he hadn't untied the mooring rope; and he had to untie it, for he hadn't a knife. He could have had four.

The rope parted at last, and he fancied he saw a dark shape close to the surface; fancied he heard the swirling noise. He sat down again and picked up the paddles. He put one between his feet and used the other, paddling first this side, then that. The boat moved sluggishly and was low at the stern. He felt water splashing over it gently. The water ran to and fro, sometimes over the tops of his shoes. He tried to go more cautiously, to keep the canoe steady. In spite of the calm surface he failed. He saw water moving sluggishly about Phiroshah's body; it seemed to be creeping up.

The mainland had seemed near; now, it was apparently as far away as it had been when he had started. Was there a current?

He kept on, his teeth still clenched tightly, breathing heavily through his nostrils. The canoe seemed to be made of lead. His feet were in water all the time now.

Light suddenly attracted him.

It moved along the trees on the mainland – the headlamps of a car. It was travelling slowly, and the beams went up and down. They turned suddenly and shone out on to the lake. Lights rippled on the water, a hundred yards away from it. The shape of another jetty and more canoes showed up; then the figures of small men climbing from the jetty into a canoe.

The headlamps went out; so did the parking lights. Only the stars gave light now.

Mannering headed towards a small island, which gave him some cover, the new development giving him temporary respite from the closer fears of the water. He watched the other boat moving swiftly, heading for the island. They would make twice the speed he was making; would quickly discover what had happened and raise an alarm. Someone would have been left in charge of the car. He paddled slowly round the sheltering island, but had a new fear – of the noise that his paddle made.

The paddle touched bottom, and the canoe swung gently round. It was pointing towards the jetty, but at least a hundred yards away. The paddle touched the bottom again and again, then the canoe shuddered as it hit mud, tipped over, and flung him to one side.

He gasped aloud.

As he grabbed the side with one hand, the other slipped and went deep into the water. He snatched it out, his heart thumping wildly. The canoe steadied, but still had a list. He sat motionless, with sweat oozing from every pore, and it was a long time before he could bring himself to move again.

They were firmly stuck. He climbed out on the landward side, and was nearly knee deep in water that seemed warm. He didn't try to pull the canoe further in, but, with his feet sinking into the mud, lifted Phiroshah and started towards land. Every step was an effort and an ordeal, but the land was near.

He reached grass.

He staggered away until he found a path with coconut palms on either side. He walked until he judged that he was nearly level with the jetty and the car, put Phiroshah down on the grass, and straightened up to ease his cramped back. He stepped through the trees and saw the shape of the car twenty yards away from him.

He edged his way towards the car, looking for a guard. He saw no one this side, and went to the other. A man was lying on the damp ground, a blanket covering him up to his chin, apparently asleep. Mannering crept nearer. The man didn't stir when Mannering hit him on the side of the jaw.

The car was an old Buick; the keys were in the ignition.

It was a nightmare drive. First along an unmade road, with the lake on one side and wooded hills on the other. At least he couldn't miss his way – there was only the one road. Then on to a gravel path which bumped him from side to side, worried him for Phiroshah; then on to tarmac, through the dark countryside, past the walking figures of the natives, past little shops where lights still burned. He didn't stop to ask the way; the road would take him somewhere.

Suddenly, the headlights shone on a signpost. He saw one finger, reading: *Bombay*.

Nearly an hour later he pulled up outside Phiroshah's bungalow.

The door opened as the car came to a standstill, and men ran down the steps, Amu and Joseph among them. They ought to be with Lorna, looking after her, thought Mannering; they oughtn't to be here. He saw Shani, then Lorna just behind her.

Shani stayed at the top of the steps, Lorna hurried down.

He called out hoarsely: "I'm all right."

He staggered out and would have fallen but for Amu's help. Lorna reached him and gripped his arm. He didn't speak to Amu, knew that the bearers were getting Phiroshah out of the back of the car. With Lorna on one side and a bearer on the other, he started up the steps. He swayed in the entrance of the hall and nearly fell again.

"Crazy," he muttered.

"You always were," Lorna said in a choky voice.

He saw Shani.

"Both of us," he said. "Your father's all right, Shani. Doctor wanted, though. I need—a drink."

"I know what you need," Lorna said.

Everything that followed was vague. The lights were too bright and hurt his eyes, but he didn't complain. Lorna and a bearer took him to a bedroom. There was a big divan bed – the most inviting bed in the world. He sat on the edge, and Lorna undressed him. A servant came in with hot soup. He had a little, waved it away, and sank back on the pillows. He had a confused mental picture of a dark tunnel and swirling water and snapping jaws.

Then he faded into sleep.

It was dark when he woke, but not with the darkness of the night. Venetian blinds were drawn at the big windows of the bedroom. A fan was whirring, but there was no other sound. The room was unfamiliar. Slowly he recalled what had happened, where he was. His mouth was dry and his head ached dully, but apart from that and stiffness he judged himself fit enough. He sat up cautiously and put a hand to his head. There was a patch of sticking-plaster.

He wondered how Phiroshah was.

He looked at the bedside table and saw a handbell of brass, inlaid with enamel. He rang it, and the tingling sound seemed too soft to reach anyone outside the room, but the door opened almost at once and Shani came in.

She wore blue. She looked young and fresh and untroubled. She smiled as she approached, and he saw a bearer moving away from her. She reached the bed and went down on her knees beside it.

"So he's all right," Mannering said.

"He will recover, with care," said Shani. "And so for the second time he owes you—"

"Forget it, please."

"How can we forget? He doesn't know what happened, but when he learns he will have a deeper gratitude than ever." She looked up into his face, and he felt the simplicity of her being.

He heard a movement, and Lorna came in, Lorna in a white linen suit, dark hair a mass of waves, eyes bright as they had ever been. Mannering felt his spirits rising. Shani stood up and went without a word. Lorna sat on the side of the bed and gripped his hands.

"All right," he said. "It could have been a lot worse."

"I suppose so. I—but you need something to eat. They seldom cook food our way here, but I've been given the run of the kitchen. Darling—"

"Hm-hm?"

"They haven't told the police. Are you going to?"

"Problem," said Mannering. He closed his eyes and pictured the scene on the island and those snapping jaws. He opened his eyes again. "Let's think about it. There isn't any hurry. Nothing else has happened, has it?"

"Nothing that matters," she said, and hurried out.

He lay back, wondering what she had meant. Then he began to wonder where he had been, where the crocodile-infested lakes were. He remembered Phiroshah asking him whether he had been known as Lucky John Mannering. He was smiling when Lorna came back with a tray. She put the tray down. To bring it in here by herself without having a bearer carry it for her was an achievement of its own.

"What's the thing that doesn't matter?" he asked.

"Oh, nothing." She grimaced at him. "Except that Imannati Patel died last night. Oh, and the son of the Maharajah of Ganpore is here and has a ridiculous idea that he's going to talk to you this morning."

CHAPTER SEVENTEEN

DR. WEINER

PATEL, who had called Mannering a fool and Phiroshah a liar, was dead. The man Phiroshah feared, the man who admitted that he was after the blue diamonds, was no longer a threat. Mannering pondered over this as he had a light breakfast and drank a lot of coffee. Lorna moved about the room, touching this, fiddling with that, trying not to break the train of his thoughts. She had recovered from the shock after Patandi's death, and was probably resigned to the fact that nothing would take Mannering away.

"Like the son of the Maharajah?" Mannering asked her.

"I haven't seen much of him," said Lorna. "He looks like an immaculate Frenchman with a dark skin. All gallantry, polish and *sang-froid*. He talks in perfect English to me and in French to Shani."

"Age?"

"It's always difficult to tell. Twenty-three or four, perhaps a year or two older."

"And I suppose they knew each other. Shani and the son of the Maharajah, I mean. What's his name, my sweet?" He finished his third cup of coffee, leaned back on the pillows and enjoyed looking at Lorna as she sat on the hide-covered pouf, hugging her knees, her head raised, and the wind from the fan ruffling her hair.

"Oh, they've met before. And his name's Jagat. J-A-G-A-T, I think."

Mannering murmured: "Could there be romance?"

"If they were English I'd make a guess, but I'm not going to try.

They hide their feelings so well. The trouble is that they all look as if they have no feeling. What made you ask?"

"A leakage at the Maharajah's palace and a leakage here," said Mannering. "Still faithful to the innocence of Shani?"

Lorna considered him almost with distaste.

"Of course I am. But I know I shouldn't be."

Mannering laughed, and a streak of pain shot through his head. He closed his eyes, heard a sound at the door, and then a murmuring. He opened his eyes a little. Joseph, with a black eye and a cut on his right cheek which looked angry and sore, was holding the door as a white man of medium height, inclined to plumpness, grey-haired and wearing glasses with thick lenses, came in breezily. He carried a brown bag. The door closed as Lorna stood up.

"Well, now, how is der invalid?" The newcomer had an accent. "Not so bad, eh?" He rubbed his hands together and smiled. He wasn't good-looking, but he had a certain breezy charm. His nose was rather too small for the rest of his face, giving him a slightly comical look. He held out his right hand. "I am Dr. Weiner. How are you, how are you?" He sat on the side of the bed and opened his case, then shook hands as if by an afterthought. "What a wonderful old man your host is, eh? Any other man of his age would be dead. Do you know how old he iss? Eighty-three. Yes, *eighty*-three. Kidnapped from his own car in a dark street, injured, and now sitting up and giving orders already. Isn't it wonderful? Now just undo der top buttons." His cool fingers had felt Mannering's pulse; he took out his stethoscope. "Now just keep quiet a minute while I see how near der grave you are." He beamed; he had small, very white teeth. "Just keep quiet." The metal top of the stethoscope wasn't really cold. "Ah, that's all right. You married an ox, Mrs. Mannering. Constitutionally, I mean – don't misunderstand me!" His accent and his manner made everything attractive. "No need to look at the head, I don't think. It will be all right if it is dressed again tomorrow. Bed, today, if you're a wise man, and if you're not, don't go running about. Now, tell me, what happened?"

Lorna said: "Dr. Weiner is a family friend of Phiro's, John."

"Ach, yes, for generations," said Weiner. "Without me, the old man wouldn't have had one of his children!" He roared with laughter. "But I must be serious." A frown wrinkled his brow alarmingly. "It is a ver' sad story. Phiroshah was proud of his children, and they were good children. Yusuf and Ali, especially. He had three favourites, now only Shani. When you help him, you help a good man."

"That's how it seemed to me," said Mannering.

"Of course—it would to any man of discernment." Weiner wrinkled his forehead again. "I told him I wouldn't let you talk to him already, but you are to tell me and I will tell him – what I think is good for him! We know about der way you were kidnapped. There is some sewage work being done on Malabar Hill. The men used a hole in the wall recently made there to catch you. The babus attacked Joseph, der men took you. They had watched you go to Phiroshah's house, here you understand, and then followed. It was a good place. After that, we know nothing."

Mannering needed to say little to make the picture vivid. He also told of the man who had fallen into the water and disappeared.

Lorna drew in an involuntary breath.

"So!" exclaimed Weiner. "Now we understand it all. You were taken to der lakes. Crocodiles by the thousand, yes. Each year one or two fishermen are taken by them. A bad place, those lakes. That island – I know it, I did not know of der caves. Not many go there; not many would know. What a lucky man you are!"

"Lucky," said Lorna unsteadily.

"Oh, I know, I know, he had to keep his wits about him to get away. Still, I say he is lucky. Yes. Now, Mannering, listen to me. You have a powerful constitution, that ox you understand, but you must have a rest. A day or two. Don't just laugh it off, my friend. I will not let young Jagat come and see you this morning." Weiner held up a hand, palm outwards. "*No*, I told him. Tonight, perhaps; tomorrow, yes – this morning, no. He will spend the day making eyes at Shani, and she will not object. This love. How do you feel, my friend? Better already? I am as good as a tonic, am I not?"

"Better," Mannering chuckled.

Weiner laughed and patted his shoulder.

"Good fellow, good chap. Oh, I forgot – your ankle – der right ankle. I looked you over last night and saw it was swollen. I bound it up, but I'd better have another look. Please. Then I must be going, or I shall be late. Remember, you are not to be foolish and do much, and if you do, that ankle might let you down." He watched Lorna unpin the elastic bandage. "Oh, not bad, not bad. A hot-water bath, then the bandage; your wife can do that for you." He prodded. "That hurt already?"

"No."

"Don't do anything to make it hurt," warned Weiner. "Now! Anything you want to ask me?" His eyes twinkled behind his glasses. "I know everything! I have been in Bombay thirty-one years, so if I don't, who does?"

Mannering murmured: "Imannati Patel?"

"Oh, to be sure. Phiroshah mentioned him." Weiner scowled. "I should not speak ill of the dead, but there is a bad man. Ach, so bad! This morning, I could hear the sigh of relief all over Bombay. Even the beggars smiled. Fonny that, you know. Parsees are big business men, astute men, a lot of them rich, but—mostly good. I would say, mostly very good. This one – when he is on der tower tomorrow and der vultures peck until his bones fall down, then there will be the end of a very bad man."

Dr. Weiner was a friend of Phiroshah.

"Ask anyone," said Weiner, and scarred his forehead again with deep furrows. "Just anyone. Phiroshah is all that is good; Patel was all that is bad. But I am late already." He jumped up.

"What does Jagat want?" Mannering asked.

"There you go, refusing to rest. Don't be silly now, Mannering. How do I know what he wants? He won't talk, even to Shani." He shook hands quickly, firmly. "I will look in this afternoon when I come to see der old man. You'd better be where I leave you. Bind him to the bed, Mrs. Mannering, use chains!" He went out, laughing.

Lorna came back from the door.

"I heard him," said Mannering humbly. "I'll be as good as I can, but I think I'll see the son of the Maharajah as soon as Weiner's left the house. And I'm going for some gentle sight-seeing this afternoon."

"No, John, you ought—"

"But I must see the police station," Mannering said. "I'm told it's unique. And there's a venerable policeman named Kana, a friend of Bristow's. I might look in to see him. You wouldn't object to that, would you?"

Lorna eyed him stonily.

"Dr. Weiner was about right. I ought to chain you to the bed."

"I'll stay in tonight, and you can read to me," said Mannering meekly. "Oh, just a little thing, my sweet. Find out when Patel's funeral will be."

"You're not going to *that.*"

"Couldn't," said Mannering. "It's a deeply religious ceremony; only Parsees can get in. But his house ought to be empty during it, don't you think?"

Lorna actually laughed.

Jagat Kalda, son of the Maharajah of Ganpore, had taken Dr. Weiner at his word, had resisted the opportunity to make eyes at Shani, and had left, saying that he would be back to see Mannering at four o'clock.

At half-past two Mannering limped down the steps to one of the Daimlers, although in fact his ankle was giving no trouble and there was no need for him to limp. It would do no harm if others thought there was. Lorna helped him into the back of the car and sat beside him. Joseph sat next to the driver. After a heavy rainstorm the streets were still damp, but the sun was out again. The temporary coolness made driving pleasant, and the rain had settled the dust. When they were near Crawford Market and the narrow streets of that part of the city, rain had even subdued the smell. They drove round for three-quarters of an hour before getting out at the club. Mannering told Joseph to be back with the car in an hour's time, waited in the hall of the club while the Daimler was driven off, then had the porter send for a taxi. Fifteen minutes later he was limping along the passages of the police headquarters, with Lorna holding his arm.

Kana, Bristow's friend, was an elderly man with very dark skin, piercing brown eyes and a permanent smile. He sat behind a huge desk, with two fans working from the corners. The desk might have been at Scotland Yard, the *Súreté Nationale* – any police headquarters in the world.

Kana greeted Lorna courteously, Mannering with a twinkle in his eyes, and did not appear to notice the parcel which Mannering put on a corner of his desk.

"Yes, Mr. Mannering, the superintendent cabled me that you were going to visit us. We're delighted! He didn't say why, but you'll remedy that? Mind you, I know something about you. How much you know about precious stones, how often you have helped Scotland Yard. Now you come to help us?"

"I hate to disappoint you," murmured Mannering. "I need help."

"Then we help each other."

"You're very good. May I ask some questions about people?"

"Phiroshah?" Kana's eyes danced. "If there is any bad in that man, I retire."

"Did you know anything about Imannati Patel?"

The light died out of Kana's eyes.

"Patel, yes," he said. Even his voice changed. "Yes. That was the worst man in Bombay whom we failed to catch. How shall I say it? There is much drug-trafficking, much eating and smoking of drugs here. Illegal, of course, but – what can you do? It is everywhere. This Imannati Patel was the big supplier. I knew, we all knew, but we could never prove it – he was so clever. Now he is dead and we breathe more freely. Others will carry on, but they are not likely to be so clever."

"Who will carry on?"

Kana shrugged.

"One never knows who worked for him. That big house of his with its dirt and decay – it was filled with mystery and mysterious comings and goings. There are many entrances we don't know about. He has three sons. Two of them work in his legal business, shipping. Are they bad? I tell you, I don't know. The other left him some years ago. In disgust, I think. So I would say that those who stayed were not disgusted and will continue with his work, but we will get them. We must. My friend—" he leaned across the desk and lowered his voice—"yesterday you called to see Patandi. You remember. Soon after you left he was killed. Murdered. Yes, yes, we knew you had been there; we have eyes and we have ears. We were quickly on the scene, and they could not clean up the back room before we arrived. Everywhere, traces of cocaine. *Everywhere*. They were impregnating tobacco with it. Also chewing gum. This would be distributed to all the little shops you see – and to the betel-nut pedlars. So we raided all of Patandi's other shops and found the same, the same. This is how he worked. Behind his shops, the drugs are made edible, ready for general sale. Then through his sons and the horde of children he collected round him he sent them out into the city, the suburbs, the nearby villages. You see? It is so easy, and so hard to prevent. There are thousands upon thousands of these begging children, these runners and distributors. Already many of them are drug addicts. They being that young; the women, also. You understand?"

Mannering murmured: "Yes, I think so." Certainly he understood Patandi's terror when he had looked into the back of the shop. "Did you find anything about the Bundi?"

"Ah," said Kana softly. "This organisation of so-called patriots who rob the rich to help the poor. No, we found nothing about them. We never do. There have been vicious crimes of violence laid at their door. *Is* there a Bundi? Or is it just a name used to hide crime of a hideous kind? I do not know. It has political roots, and political intrigue is as rife today as it was yesterday. There is a new villain, that is all! You seek the Bundi?"

"They seem to be interested in some of the things that interest me."

"The more you see of Bombay the more you will understand our difficulties," said Kana. "Finding witnesses, finding evidence, that is the terrible task we have here. But we keep doing a little, and now that Patel has gone perhaps we will have a big clean-up. It may touch the Bundi, it may not. Of this Patandi – he was a distant relative of Patel's. He discovered more than most. The surprising thing was that Patel allowed him to live for so long. Perhaps because he was a relative. Who knows? The tragedy is that Patandi was one of the few men we know was directly associated with Patel. It cannot be helped, but it was a blow to us. Why are you interested in Patel?"

"I heard that, like the Bundi, he was interested in the affairs of the Maharajah of Ganpore," Mannering said. "I wanted to find out – probably Phiroshah told you I was going to Ganpore to look at the jewels."

"Yes, I knew," said Kana. "Perhaps I guess more than I know! Mr. Mannering, what is it you really want of me?"

"Do you know of any good reasons why I shouldn't go to Ganpore?" asked Mannering.

CHAPTER EIGHTEEN

DISGUISE FOR ONE

KANA frowned and didn't answer at once. Mannering glanced at Lorna, who was still looking out of the window.

Kana moved his hands, a little gesture of uncertainty.

"I know of none. Ganpore is a long way from everywhere, it is buried. There has been little attempt to interfere with it, and the Maharajah is still the ruler although now responsible to the All India Government. If you go, fly. The journey by road or by train is long, weary, dirty. Mrs. Mannering would not enjoy it. But if Patel was interested, there could be something I do not know about," said Kana. "Are you sure?"

"He tried to stop me from going."

"So! He was up to his tricks, and that makes you wonder if he was one of the Bundi. That could be. But understand, Ganpore is not in my jurisdiction. It comes under Calcutta. There is a State Police Force, which seldom calls for help outside. It would not be possible for me to do anything to help, unless requested by the Maharajah, or instructed by Calcutta. They might, if they knew that Patel had been involved; but would they know? Have I answered you, my friend? Have I made it clear that Ganpore is cut off from everywhere?"

"Very clear," said Mannering. "And I'm very grateful."

"To be of assistance to a friend of Bristow – what more can I ask?" Kana said. "Or, for that matter, to an Englishman. Yes, I am one of the many who regret the passing of the British Raj. Here, in the police especially, we are the poorer for their going. Please don't quote me!" He smiled and stood up. "Your parcel, don't forget it."

"Your parcel," Mannering said. "With Bill Bristow's good wishes. Barley sugar, I believe."

Kana beamed, thanked and ushered them to the door.

Joseph was at the club, and the Mannerings went ahead of him to Phiroshah's bungalow. It was half-past four.

Amu was on the steps, as if waiting.

"Hallo," said Mannering, limping exaggeratedly. "Is Jagat here?"

"No, sahib; he has not returned." There was a hint of anxiety in his voice and his manner. "He came at two o'clock. Shani went out with him. They were to be back, to see you, at four o'clock. They will not be long."

"I'll see them as soon as they come in," said Mannering. 'That's if Jagat hasn't changed his mind!" He went to the room which had been designated for them. Lorna took off her hat and poked her fingers through hair damp from the humid warmth. "Pity it doesn't rain again."

Lorna didn't answer.

"Tea or fruit juice?" asked Mannering.

"I'd like a long gin!"

"We should have gone to the Taj," said Mannering.

"Or to the airport, for the London plane."

"Still like that?"

"Didn't Kana terrify you? With warnings about an isolated state and no outside police control? He wanted to scare you in a nice way."

"I doubt it – he just wanted me to know what we might be up against."

"I had a feeling that he wanted you to go," Lorna admitted.

"He probably thinks I'll blunder into something which would simplify his problems. I wonder what Jagat wants."

"You weren't far wrong about him and Shani."

Mannering grinned. "Second sight!"

"Was it just a guess?"

"I suppose so." Mannering rang the bell, and asked for tea and iced drinks when Amu appeared.

"Yes, sahib."

"Are the others back?"

"Not yet, sahib."

"Were they alone?"

"His Highness's bearer followed, sahib, but His Highness drove his own car."

"And they're nearly an hour late."

"That is so." Amu moved backwards towards the door. "They will be here soon." He spoke as if he was trying to convince himself.

Neither Jagat nor Shani was back by eight o'clock that night, but old Phiroshah wasn't told.

When the Mannerings, Joseph and Amu reached the Taj Mahal Hotel at ten o'clock there was still no news. Lorna had a shower and went to bed. Mannering read until midnight; there was no word.

There was no news of the missing couple next morning.

Lorna, with her hair spread over the pillow and her cheeks flushed from sleep, watched Mannering for a while, then said quietly: "They could have eloped."

"But kidnapping's in fashion."

"I suppose there isn't a chance of making you go home, even if they've been kidnapped."

Mannering leaned over her. "Not a chance, my optimist. The only question is whether to take you to Ganpore or leave you here."

"I'm coming," said Lorna.

A worried Amu was outside the door of the bedroom when Mannering went out just after ten. The tall Hindu bearer had become almost part of their lives.

"Before I went to the lakes," Mannering said, "I had arranged to see an expert in disguise. Do you know who it was?"

"Yes, sahib."

"Do you trust him?"

"With my life, sahib."

"Can you arrange a meeting this afternoon?"

"At what time, sahib?"

"As soon as you can, after two," said Mannering.

He left just after two, with Joseph as guide, leaving Amu to look after Lorna. They went by taxi into the heart of the city, past the teeming masses, the swarming beggars, the itinerant salesmen, the colour and the squalor. Mannering looked about him, hardly noticing what he saw.

The taxi stopped in a narrow, quiet street of Western-type houses, but at the end of the street was a camp for refugees from the winter's floods; acre upon acre of land filled with tiny tents, mostly made of banana or palm fronds thrown over sticks which held them up. Mannering saw the families living in the dirt, over-crowded in a way revolting to Western eyes. The wind came from the camp and sickened him.

"We walk, please," Joseph said.

Mannering limped, and kept his right hand in his pocket about his gun. They reached smaller houses, built in the Indian style, and Joseph stood aside for Mannering to enter an open doorway. The passage was narrow and dark; the smell of spices and Indian food was thick and heavy.

"Here, sahib."

Mannering went into a darkened room, but Joseph switched on a light. Fluorescent strip lighting flickered, then became bright.

A middle-aged Hindu in spotless dhoti and spotless linen coat and turban bowed slightly and smiled.

"You are welcome, sahib. I am Alaka Chopra, at your service." His voice was high-pitched, his English seemed to come with an effort, but the accent was good. "1 understand you wish to disguise yourself."

"As a Sikh, if that is practicable."

"It is the only wise way." Chopra was reassuring. "Already Mr. Phiroshah has told me, and I have clothes ready. You understand that you will need to eat Indian food when you are with others. You will have to learn the habits quickly. I am prepared to teach you, but it will take time. Two three days – after that, you will know just a little. If you take Amu or Joseph with you, they can always be of assistance, but you understand—" he smiled deprecatingly—"that it is not a simple matter of the face, the figure, the clothes. It is complicated. And I understand you wish to be able to remove the disguise yourself, also to put it on yourself afterwards."

"In emergency, yes."

"The difficulty will be to look today as you were yesterday. If it can be avoided, do not change the final disguise. Now—please sit here."

There was a swivel chair, a barber's mirror and a big barber's smock. Mannering sat down. Chopra went to a large suitcase and took out his equipment. Grease-paint, a beard, a wig, a dozen different things. Joseph stood silently by the door.

Mannering submitted to the gentle hands and firm movements of the youthful-looking Hindu, and watched himself change in front of his eyes.

Nearly an hour later Mannering stood in front of a long mirror and studied the reflection of the Sikh; he did not recognise himself. The greasepaint had altered his complexion to the tawny brown of the hardy men of the hills; the shape of his eyes and cheeks was different. He had a small dark beard which curled a little, hair that seemed to grow low on the nape of his neck. The turban concealed his own hair; the clothes gave his body a different shape. He wore a long khaki tunic, knee breeches and puttees, with pointed, turned-up toes. The puttees were hot but there was no way of avoiding them. He studied himself closely, then turned to his own make-up case.

He took out everything he needed to clean off the disguise, and worked while the men watched, without comment; Chopra obviously disapproved.

In twenty minutes the transformation was gone, except for the clothes.

Chopra didn't speak.

Mannering hitched the chair closer to the mirror and set to work – deft touches with greasepaint, everything he needed. Gradually, very gradually, he turned into the Sikh. He took longer than Chopra, but as he worked he saw the Hindu watching with an astonishment he couldn't hide. All disapproval faded.

He finished.

Chopra said softly: 'That is remarkable, Mr. Mannering. I would not have thought it possible. If only you knew the language!"

"I'll manage," Mannering said. "Joseph and Amu will talk for me. Joseph, I want you to take that case back to the hotel. Tell the memsahib I shall be late, but she is not to worry. Tell her I am just trying out my new clothes."

"Yes, sahib. Can I tell you where it is best to go?"

"I know where to go," said Mannering.

He didn't add that he was going to the home of the late Imannati Patel.

CHAPTER NINETEEN

FORCED ENTRY

MANNERING reached the end of Woodham Road at dusk. He had walked from Chopra's house, and his ankle wasn't as sound as he had expected it to be. No one had given him a second glance, not even the Sikhs he had passed on the way. He went briskly past No. 81. Dim lights shone at two downstairs windows, none upstairs.

He turned back and went into the drive of the house next door. Halfway along, a gap in the hedge was large enough to squeeze through. He stepped on to the drive of Patel's house, looking at the lighted windows, then up at the starlit sky. He moved quietly towards the back of the house, but saw no light.

He had a roll of tools and the gun. He pulled on a pair of cotton gloves, then tried the handle of the back door; it was locked. The windows were both locked and shuttered. Standing close to the door, he listened intently, but heard nothing. He took out a pick-lock and slipped it into the keyhole.

He heard metal scraping on metal. In less than thirty seconds the lock clicked back smoothly.

He opened the door, and there was no light.

He stepped inside.

As the door closed behind him and he stood in the darkness, years seemed to slip away. He wasn't in India; he was disguised, but not as a burly Sikh. He was the Baron, cracksman extraordinary, standing on the threshold of a house where the owner slept, and where jewels worth a fortune waited for the taking. He was the man

Bristow had hunted throughout England, and whom the French police had sought in Paris and in Lyons.

He took a slim pencil torch from the pocket of his tunic and shone it round.

The smell of spices had already told him he was in the kitchen – a small room. Another door was opposite, and as the torchlight shone through it he saw that it led to the passage which ran alongside the stairs. He stepped out and saw a faint light beneath a door on the right. He went forward soundlessly.

He reached the foot of the stairs.

The other light he had seen from the garden came from a room on the left of the stairs. There were rooms on either side, and he hesitated before stepping towards the front door. He opened then closed it again. The catch was easy to slip, and in emergency he could get out that way.

He went back to the stairs and opened the door on the right stealthily. He peered in. Two men sat on upright chairs, facing each other; neither was talking, and he thought that one was asleep. Both were dressed in European clothes. He crept out and opened the other door.

Several sari-clad women sat on cushions on the floor, all of them looking towards the carpet. They were beautifully dressed. The silence of meditation made a hush about the room. Mannering closed the door gently and went up to the room where he had seen Patel.

The only light here was from his torch.

He shone it towards the floor, remembering the way a man had squatted in the corner, remembering how servants rolled themselves up in their blankets and slept on the boards. Were eyes straining at him in the darkness? He found his way to Patel's room, wondered if the police had been here yet; he saw no traces of a search.

He studied photographs on the dressing-table and other pieces of furniture, then went to the room where the servant in the corner had startled him.

The man wasn't there.

Mannering shone the torch round slowly, carefully, keeping the beam below the level of the window, and drew the curtains. He smelt a delicate perfume he had noticed before. He closed the door and switched on the light. The room was shabby. The striped wallpaper with the flowered design reminded him of some of the faded salons of Paris. So did the Louis Quinze furniture; part of the house was furnished as Indians would furnish it, but most was Westernised. There was a large double bed.

A cord hung from one of the posts, the kind of cord which had been used to bind him in the cave. It had been cut, and the cut was clean. At the other side of the bed there was nothing, but more cord lay on the floor beneath the post. It was in two half-circles, showing where it had been cut from the wrists of someone who had been tied to the post.

Had Shani and the Maharajah's son been tied up here?

The perfume reminded him of Shani. He turned to the door. A piece of blue material, silk which might have come from a sari, had caught in the barrel of the lock. Shani had worn blue that day. He ran the piece of silk between his gloved fingers, then put it in his pocket.

He searched every drawer in Patel's room and found many papers, most of them written in English, a few in Hindu or a language with Indian characters. The Indian writing showed how heavily the dice were loaded against him. He studied the photographs again, then turned towards the door of the room which had been empty.

The light shone on emptiness, at first – then on to a chair – then on to a man sitting in the chair.

Mannering kept the light steady on the man's legs. He was dressed in European clothes. He wasn't moving. Mannering listened with bated breath, but could not hear the sound of another's breathing. He raised the light, slowly. It fell on a grey suit. It fell on a young face, an olive-coloured chin and on to dark eyes, which were wide open, staring; the light hardly made the other man blink.

Jagat? He was sure it was.

Jagat was bound hand and foot to the chair, and a cloth was tied round his mouth, gagging him.

Words sprang to Mannering's lips but he kept them back. He was a Sikh who hadn't the power of speech, and had to remember that. The youth could only see his shape. The light was shining into his face, half blinding him.

Mannering didn't put on the room light.

He put the torch on a pouf so that it shone on a level with Jagat's waist, and took out a sheathed knife, part of his props. He cut the cords at the youngster's ankles and wrists, then removed the gag. Jagat slumped in his chair, but couldn't get up at once. Mannering began to massage his wrists, then his ankles. Jagat kept hissing, as if against pain.

That was the only sound. None came from outside or downstairs.

Mannering worked swiftly, desperately; they might be interrupted at any minute. He couldn't guess how long it would be before Jagat could move freely. After a long ten minutes, Jagat grunted as he tried to get up, held the chair tightly and managed to get to his feet.

Mannering wanted to tell him what to do, but didn't know a word of Hindi, daren't speak in English, because the day would come when Jagat might recognise him. Jagat began to move, and they walked round the room several times, until Jagat could stand without help.

Jagat spoke in whispers, in a language Mannering didn't understand. He didn't answer. Jagat whispered again, more insistently. Mannering shook his head, but the faint light probably hid that from the youngster. He made a queer sound in his throat, as a dumb man might do. Jagat stopped whispering, and walked about again, then went towards the door.

Mannering switched off the torch.

Jagat might try to avenge himself; might cause trouble; or might have the sense to sneak out. Mannering wasn't sure, but knew what he wanted. Jagat made little sound as he crept out of the room and across Patel's bedroom towards the stairs. Mannering now shone the torch behind him so that he could see.

Jagat reached the stairs, turned and looked at the light, and beckoned. Mannering stood still. Jagat went down, making hardly a sound. Mannering gave him time to reach the front door, then followed to the head of the stairs.

He saw a light from outside; Jagat was opening the door, going out furtively.

The door closed.

Mannering put out the torch again. He had no papers, nothing else that would help. If he were wise, he would go now, but – he hadn't found the safe.

Would it be downstairs?

He returned to Patel's room, locked each door, put out the light and went to the window. Outside there was a ledge almost immediately beneath him, then a long drop to the ground. The only near tree was a phoenix palm; he knew the sharp, sword-like fronds too well to take chances with those trees. But if he reached the ledge and hung from it, he could drop to the ground with reasonable safety.

He closed the window, went to the main door and switched on the light.

In this very room of death he stood and studied the walls, the furniture placed against them in studied disorder. One big chest was in a different place from when he had first seen it; so was a large dressing-table, a mahogany piece, incongruous here. He went across and moved the chest, then the dressing-table.

It was as simple as that.

The safe was built into the wall.

The Baron knelt in front of the safe, his tools spread out by his side, drilling. The noise of the drill was soft but persistent. Every minute or so he paused to listen, and heard no other sound. Tiny iron filings curled out from the holes he was making round the lock. It was an old-fashioned safe; easy to open unless there were some refinements which Patel had fitted specially.

He had been working for twenty minutes before he was able to lift out the lock.

There was no trick fastening; he opened the door of the safe without trouble. Inside were two shelves, each of them filled, mostly with documents. There were several jewel-cases, and there was also a packet wrapped in brown paper. He took the packet out first, broke it open and found white powder; this was probably cocaine. He put it aside and opened a jewel-case. The diamond necklace inside was a beautiful thing, worth a small fortune, but not unique and of no special interest to the Baron.

He opened another.

Blue diamonds winked up at him.

CHAPTER TWENTY

MORE DIAMONDS

THERE were twelve diamonds in this case, each fitted into a groove in the velvet cushion. Mannering laid it aside, and opened another, larger case; there were thirty gems, looking exactly the same. A third case held nine.

Mannering carried the smallest case close to the light, took out one gem and studied it closely. Then he went back to the safe and took out the white diamond necklace. One stone was cut with sharper edges than most. He used this edge to scrape the side of a blue diamond; he hardly touched it, just pressed and twisted, then examined the blue gem again.

He could see where the real diamond had marked it; this was paste.

He tested the rest of the nine blue gems; they were all the same. He wanted time to make sure of every one, but was getting restless. If Jagat had taken the normal course, the police would soon be on the way. There were two risks of being interrupted.

Mannering opened the window again; everything was normal outside.

He tested blue gem after blue gem, and all were easily scratched by the real diamond. Fifty-one paste stones were here, each looking identical with the genuine blue diamond which Phiroshah had sent him.

He put them all back in their cases, tucked them under his arm, and went to the window. Everything was as he had seen it before.

He put the tools back in the canvas roll, and slipped this round his waist; it didn't impede him or make a bulge. Then he lifted a corner of the dressing-table and let it drop heavily.

The boards of the room shook.

He paused; a door downstairs opened and men spoke, footsteps sounded on the stairs, then running footsteps. He made for the window and climbed out, dropping one of the jewel-cases inside the room. Someone had reached the door and thudded on it, someone else called out in Hindi. Mannering climbed to the ledge and dropped another case, into the room. He heard it open, heard the paste gems rolling about.

The door groaned as someone thudded against it.

He bent down so that his hands and feet rested on the ledge then put one leg over and got to his knees. He heard the door burst open and men rush into the room. He eased his knees off the ledge, and hung full length; the third jewel-case fell into the garden. He saw the face of a man appear at the window.

Mannering dropped.

As he dropped, he heard something hit against the ground and saw a flash of silver light. A knife tore at his tunic. He bent his knees to take the strain, dropped more heavily on his left foot that his right, yet the right hurt him. He turned left and ran. Another silver flash passed him, and a knife stuck into the wooden gate-post.

There was neither shooting nor shouting.

He ran towards the nearest corner, turned and began to slow down. He was walking quickly when a gharry came along.

"Taj Mahal," Mannering said in a way which he hoped sounded like the Hindi pronunciation, and climbed into the gharry. He couldn't see out, there was no window in the hood. He didn't try to look out at the sides. The driver gently whipped his horse to a brisker walk. Nothing else happened. Cars passed, people walked swiftly and silently by. When they turned a corner, Mannering looked round.

There was no sign of pursuit.

Mannering climbed out of the gharry, paid the man double his fare without arguing, without saying a word. The hotel was so big that there was a good chance that he wouldn't be noticed. He reached his own floor by the stairs. Joseph was standing with his infinite patience outside the main door. Joseph saw him and stiffened.

"All well," Mannering said. "Open the door."

"Yes—yes, sahib." Joseph had seen him when he left, but was startled.

"No one has come in, do you understand?"

"Yes, sahib."

Mannering slipped through into the empty outer room.

Joseph closed the door, and Mannering stopped in the middle of the room, breathing heavily, wiping his forehead. He had never felt so hot. He started to move towards the door of the drawing-room, when it opened.

Lorna came out, glanced up and stopped abruptly. She didn't speak, but went pale. Then she backed a pace, and said sharply: "Who are you?"

"Spare a copper, lidy," said Mannering.

She exclaimed: "John!" She backed another pace, but the quick surge of fear had gone. "You—brute!"

"Like me?"

"It's perfect. You look dreadful."

"Well, you married me."

"Not in that outfit. I—" She stopped, drew nearer, peered at him closely, and realised at once that he hadn't come simply to show himself off. "What's—what's happened?"

"Nothing that won't help. Heard anything from Phiroshah's house?"

"They're not back," said Lorna.

Mannering did not speak.

"Amu telephoned," Lorna continued. "Phiroshah knows. He wants to see you."

"I'll go as soon as I can," said Mannering. "I must get this stuff off. Joseph has seen me, so there's no need to worry about him." He led the way to the bedroom. "Think you could rustle up a cup of coffee?"

"I've some orange juice," said Lorna.

She telephoned for coffee as he stripped down to singlet and trunks. The fans gave some coolness. He sat at the dressing-table with the make-up beside him, started to work, and sighed: "Oh, for a real drink!"

"We can get permits, but it's hardly worth it," said Lorna. "Bombay's the only dry province; you can get anything you want outside."

"Life can begin again in Ganpore." Mannering was cleaning his face. The beard and the false hair were on the dressing-table with the turban. There was a tap at the door, and Lorna hurried to take the tray. Mannering was nearly finished when she came in, with the coffee poured. He sat back against the dressing-table and took a sip. He looked up, startled.

"What's *this*?"

"Coffee," said Lorna blandly.

He sipped again, and a rapt expression crossed his face. He drank slowly, relishing every mouthful.

"Best coffee I've ever tasted," he pronounced. "I'll have some more. You were right, you see. You're nearly always right."

"I wish you meant it," said Lorna feelingly. "Amu brought a bottle of brandy and a bottle of Scotch. We have to hide it, and mustn't produce it if we have any Indian visitors. Will you have a straight drink, now?"

"I'll have a bath first." Mannering hurried to the bathroom. Lorna kept the door open, and he talked above the splashing of the shower. "Anything else turned up?"

"Phiroshah had a message—at least, his servants did. He's been told that if he says anything to the police he won't see Shani again. The amazing thing—" She stopped.

"Yes?"

"He takes it so—calmly. Stoically."

"Seen him?"

"Weiner let me, for five minutes."

"I must say I like the doctor," said Mannering, towelling steadily. "Want to know what I've been up to?"

"Oh no," said Lorna. "What makes you think I'd be interested?" She poured him out a whisky, adding a splash of soda as he came into the bedroom. He sipped and began to dress, talking casually. Lorna sat in a long chair, with a fan stirring her hair, watching, nodding occasionally.

"Of course I could have brought the paste things with me, but I thought it would be a nice touch to leave them behind, as if by accident."

"Brilliant," said Lorna icily. "If you've really gone mad."

"The madness being?"

"If you'd taken them, you could have stopped a substitution. That's obviously what they're planning to do. I can't see why—"

"Sorry," murmured Mannering humbly. "Must have been a mental black-out. Had a queer notion that I'd rather let them carry on with the plan. After all, they'll have to do it at Ganpore, won't they? So they're going to Ganpore with the fifty-one paste diamonds. The thing to do is catch 'em in the switch. Really crazy?"

"Not if you catch them, I suppose," Lorna conceded.

"Thing is," said Mannering, fully dressed and sitting back in a cane long chair, "supposing they were known to have these replicas. The crime doesn't begin until they start to pretend they're the real ones. With the auction coming off at Ganpore, that's the obvious place for the switch. No thief in his senses would have left the stones there on purpose – how could a poor thief know they were paste? He'd naturally think they were real and try to get off with them. Luckless chap drops them in the chase, wicked men get them back and thank their stars. What more convincing can you want?"

"I suppose you're right." Lorna wasn't convinced.

"Come here, my sweet." He stood up, and she moved in front of him. He slipped his hand into his pocket. "Head forward." She obeyed. He put the necklace of real diamonds round her neck, fastened the catch, kissed the top of her head, and said: "Go and look in the mirror."

She swung round. Diamonds scintillated with the beauty of fire and colour. She stared at them, touching them almost fearfully, then looked at Mannering's reflection in the mirror, as he came behind her.

"Pretty," he said casually.

"John, you *fool*!"

"Oh, my sweet! A poor thief I would have seemed if I'd left everything behind. Oh no. I tucked the real stuff safely away. Any thief knows that ordinary diamonds are worth a fortune, but might not be impressed by the blue ones, so he'd naturally make sure of the money." He laughed. "Yes, they suit you."

Lorna's eyes stormed.

"Bristow would say—"

"The bold, bad Baron!" Mannering chuckled. "One day, we'll tell him all about it. Of course, you don't have to keep them. Throw them in my face. Or ask Phiroshah whether he can identify them, they're probably stolen. Be as well to let him take care of them, anyhow. Still, they're nice."

Lorna took them off, held them in her hands for a moment, fascinated by their fire. She was smiling.

"Darling," she said, "you ought to have stayed a jewel-thief. I can't imagine what changed you, you do it all so well. We'll send these anonymously to Kana, if you don't mind."

"What a way to clear our consciences! It'll be done. Odd thing, by the way. Jagat – I suppose it was Jagat! – didn't go rushing to the police, as you might have expected. I don't think the men at Patel's place did, either. They threw knives about like circus performers, but they didn't use guns and they didn't shout 'Stop, thief'. I—what's worrying you?"

"They *threw* knives!"

"Very blunt," said Mannering, "and very indifferent throwers. They wouldn't hold an audience for five minutes." He took the diamonds from her and put them beneath some clothes in a drawer of the dressing-table, came back into the drawing room and asked: "Have a drink?"

"I need one badly." She watched him pour out. "What are you going to do next?"

"Wait," said Mannering firmly. "Weiner told me I had to rest, didn't he ? Not that I think there'll be a lot of time for resting or waiting. Unless Jagat is playing a remarkably odd game, we'll hear from him soon."

The telephone bell rang.

Mannering looked at the instrument thoughtfully, but went to it before Lorna could move. He lifted the receiver slowly, and she knew that thoughts were racing through his mind; she wished she knew what thoughts.

"John Mannering here," he said. "Yes . . ."

"Oh, yes," he repeated.

"Yes," he said. "Right away." He put down the receiver and beamed across at her. "Jagat's on his way; we should hear something worth knowing soon."

CHAPTER TWENTY-ONE

THE SON OF THE MAHARAJAH

AMU opened the door.

Jagat Kalda of Ganpore came in, and Mannering saw him in a good light for the first time. He was neither tall nor short, had a figure no one could complain about – not lean, certainly not fat. His grey suit fitted him perfectly. His eyes were a little bloodshot and there were puffy marks at the corners of his lips. His dark hair was wavy but brushed sleekly back from his forehead; he was almost too handsome.

"Mrs. Mannering." He bowed. "Mr. Mannering. I am sorry that I am so late."

"Hardly your fault," murmured Mannering.

Jagat shrugged.

"It was wholly my fault. Had I stayed and waited to see you, instead of being impatient and spending the afternoon attempting to amuse myself and Shani this would not have happened. Mr. Mannering—I am frightened for her."

"You're not the only one," said Mannering.

"I heard the man who captured us and I can imagine, perhaps more than you. I have tried to reassure her father, to tell him that we were well treated. That is not true." He moved about the drawing-room as he talked restlessly; he looked very young. "It is a miracle that I escaped. A man broke into the house – Imannati Patel's house – and freed me. Unhappily, Shani had been taken away before that. I dared to hope that she was also free, but—" He broke off, shrugging, despondent. "I do not know where she is. Her father is in great distress. I am—frightened; and Shani is in grave danger. We need your help, Mr. Mannering."

"Police?" asked Mannering mildly.

"But there has been the message that if any report is made to the police then she will be in worse danger. This is not a matter we can discuss with the police. Had it been, I should have gone to them immediately I was freed."

Mannering said: "I see."

"You disagree? You think that the police should be informed?"

"I think we ought to try every way to find Shani."

"But not to make her situation worse." Jagat was obviously holding himself on a tight leash. "There is nothing I will not do to find her."

"Do you know why she was kidnapped?"

"But of course." Jagat stood in front of Mannering – a little too close. "She was with me and she is the daughter of Aly Phiroshah. Each was a sufficient reason."

Mannering moved away, sat on the arm of a chair, looked at the youngster s calmly, wondered what storms were really raging in his mind.

"Was it?" Mannering took out cigarettes. "I don't understand why."

"You *know* the story."

"I know about the attempts to steal the one blue diamond, and the murder of Phiroshah's two sons," said Mannering. "Have you the other diamonds with you?"

"*With* me?" Jagat looked as if he wondered whether he were talking to a fool. "They are at Ganpore with my father. They are to be sold – if we can keep them long enough." There was bitterness in his voice. "I am beginning to wonder. There is no doubt why I was kidnapped; it is surely obvious. I was told that my father would be informed, and that he would ransom me – with the blue diamonds. Phiroshah was also to be told that he could ransom his daughter. That is enough, surely. The problem is to find out who is behind it. Is it the Bundi? I came with a message for you from my father. We need your help."

"Ah, yes," Mannering said.

"It is a message I am reluctant to deliver. That my father—" Jagat paused, raised his hands, looked as if he could hardly bring himself to speak. When he did, the words came swiftly. "My father asks me to tell you that he has reason to doubt the honesty of old Aly Phiroshah. I have reasoned with him, argued with him, but he has those doubts. I was to warn you. I was to ask you to come with me to Ganpore, but not to tell the old man when you were leaving. It is my father's opinion that Phiroshah will endeavour to stop you."

"Oh," said Mannering blankly.

He saw Lorna move and hoped that she wouldn't speak.

"I don't get it," he said at last. "Why doubt the man who brought me? Why should he go to the trouble of bringing me if he is going to prevent me from going to Ganpore?"

"I think it is folly," Jagat said, "but—that is the message. You can understand now why I had to give it to you in person and could not pass it on to anyone else. Until I arrived here, I would not believe it. I am dutiful, I must be, and I came as a special envoy, but—I was sceptical. Angry. But now—"

"Yes?" asked Mannering almost lazily.

"Can't *you* see? An attempt was made to prevent me from giving you the message. Phiroshah could have done that. Yes, Phiroshah knew where I was going. It would be clever to have Shani kidnapped too. Would a man kidnap his own daughter? Yes, if he knew that she was not in danger."

Mannering stubbed out his cigarette.

"Yet you're frightened for Shani."

"I fear what will happen to her if she should discover that her father is a rogue, a murderer. Oh, I hardly know what I am saying. Mannering, will you come to Ganpore?"

Mannering didn't answer.

"Will you come?"

Mannering took out a fresh cigarette.

"Are the other dealers there?"

"Yes. They are guests of my father. He has told them that he will have the blue diamonds for them to examine tomorrow. If we fly, we can be there in time. If necessary he will delay for another day—two days. He is anxious for you to be there. He knows of your reputation."

"Who told him?"

Jagat hesitated.

"Who told him?"

"Phiroshah," Jagat said.

"Explain his faith in me, if he thinks Phiroshah a rogue."

"I do not attempt to explain it. I can only tell you what my father says. I repeat, he is anxious that you should leave here without telling Phiroshah or anyone else. It can be arranged. I came by air – I fly my own aircraft. I am a fully qualified pilot. Or we could charter a plane from one of the companies. The important thing is that you leave for Ganpore quickly. The transport can be arranged with an hour's notice."

"No," said Mannering. "Not tonight. In the morning."

Jagat said: "If nothing will change your mind, then I must accept that. But you will say nothing to Phiroshah or to anyone?"

"No," said Mannering deliberately.

"When shall I meet you?"

"At the airport," Mannering said, "at ten o'clock tomorrow morning."

"You will be alone?"

"Yes."

Lorna stirred again, but didn't speak.

"I will telephone my father," Jagat said.

Mannering saw him to the outer door of the suite, with Amu standing and watching. Mannering lit a cigarette as he heard the lift doors close, and was smiling faintly when he returned to the drawing-room. Lorna, sitting in an easy chair, looked at him through her lashes.

"*Very* funny," she said. "What are you up to now?"

"Impressed by him?"

"He's a hopeless liar."

"Hopeless?" asked Mannering.

"Some of his story was palpably untrue. The only possible reason for slandering Phiroshah like that is to get you to Ganpore without Phiroshah knowing. Goodness knows why. For a man who pretends to be fond of Shani—"

Mannering laughed.

"Shani is lucky in some of her friends, anyhow! But spend a little more time on Jagat, my sweet. He's a Hindu of the highest caste. The humblest of them are adept at concealing their feelings; so is he. Yet he preferred to make them obvious. He doubts his father at least as much as he doubts Phiroshah, and told me so. I wonder why."

"I only know that I didn't like the young man."

"And hope Shani comes to her senses!"

Lorna stood up quickly. "John, Shani *is* missing."

"Oh yes," said Mannering. "But we'll find her, and we won't find that her father was party in the plot to kidnap her. Do you think you'd look well in a sari?"

Lorna stared.

"Of course you're not quite the figure for it, they're best without foundation garments," said Mannering, "but I think you'd get by. Just to slip out of the hotel, without being recognised. I'll turn into my Sikh again, so we'll both get out. Tonight. Or are you too tired?"

"What on earth are you thinking up now?" said Lorna.

"We'll go to Ganpore before anyone expects us," said Mannering. "Why not surprise everyone, including Jagat? You can borrow a sari. You'll have to draw your hair tightly back from your forehead and try to get it straight. Notice how none of the Indian women have curly hair, but all the men seem to have it? Well, most of the men."

"I don't have to borrow a sari. I bought a beautiful one while I was out with Shani, and some sandals. I'd have shown them to you, but you've been too busy. I suppose you are serious."

"Very," said Mannering.

"Aren't you going to tell anyone?"

"No one at Phiroshah's house. It's almost a pity I changed." Mannering looked at the telephone longingly. "I don't think that I could trust that; I'll slip out for half an hour." He chuckled at her expression. "Sorry, my sweet. Call it an impulse. I won't be long."

"Where are you going?"

"For once in my life I'm going to be sensible. I'm going to talk to Kana the Policeman."

"This is unexpected, my friend, but no less a pleasure." Kana greeted Mannering in a small room in his house at the foot of Malabar Hill. Dressed in a dhoti and turban he was hardly recognisable as the little man in European clothes who had welcomed them at the police headquarters. "How can I help you?"

Mannering was sitting on the only chair in the room, where tapestries hung on the walls.

"First, I need a small aircraft that can take me and two passengers to Ganpore."

Kana raised his hands. "That is simply a matter of a telephone call. Yes?"

"Then I need a bearer, who will be the third passenger. My wife and I are going."

"A policeman?"

"Preferably not. It may be unofficial. At least, a man who can be discreet – almost as discreet as you."

Kana showed his fine teeth.

"Yes, that can be done without great difficulty. And what else?"

"I might find it necessary to be in possession of stolen jewels," Mannering said. "Temporary possession. I might even be accused of stealing them. In fact, I shall turn them over to you – if I find them in my pockets. You'll look after them, won't you?"

"I am sure that could be arranged," said Kana. He took an envelope out of the folds of his dhoti. "Here is a licence to carry firearms good for all India. I hope you won't have to use it, but it is as well to be safe, isn't it? Good luck, my friend."

They left the hotel, wearing their Indian clothes, but Mannering without heavy facial disguise. They met Kana's man, changed in a small house he took them to, then took a taxi to the airport. No one could report that they had left the hotel.

CHAPTER TWENTY-TWO

GANPORE

BELOW them the land was parched and arid. Above, the sun burned. They had flown through a night of stars. There had been no rain; and here it seemed as if rain never came. Only twice during the day had they seen a river. In the middle of each there had been a trickle of water; the rest was dry, cracked river-bed, with a little pale green growth near it.

They had passed over great cities, the colour and the squalor of which was hidden from the air. They had watched the mule trains and the ox-waggons plodding their way from city to city, village to village.

Ahead of them a range of hills rose out of the plain.

The pilot, a young Sikh, had said very little during the journey. Their bearer, Ramdhal, had passable English. They climbed above the hills. On the other side it was like being transported to a different world. The lower slopes were grass-clad; small rivers flowed criss-cross and meandered through fertile valleys and small plains. To the west a vast area was almost under water – rice fields, Ramdhal had said. Ganpore, being isolated, was almost self-supporting in food.

There were several small towns and innumerable villages; only the town of Ganpore was really large. The palace was two miles to the west of the town. They would see it from the air, Ramdhal had assured them. Yes, he had once been to Ganpore; he had worked there for two years.

At last they saw the town, spreading over a great area of the countryside. A river ran through it, and the sun glistened on the surface, turning it to gold.

Mannering picked out the palace, a square white building, standing out against the land; not far from it a smaller building, which seemed to sparkle as if the walls were studded with jewels.

Ramdhal said: "The palace, sahib—and the tomb."

"Ah, yes," said Mannering.

The plane was losing height. The airfield was nearer the palace than the town, and they could see the two runways; only small planes could land and take off. Mannering sat back and fastened his belt. Ramdhal scorned that. He was tall for a Hindu, powerful, rather like a Sikh to look at, with fine features and piercing eyes. He wore a white jacket and white trousers and a black fez cap – a bearer's dress which would pass anywhere.

A few men stood about the small airport building. The aircraft landed smoothly, and taxied near the Indians, who moved slowly towards it while others watched from the side of the field. Oxen lumbered along a nearby road, two to each of seven carts with wheels which were nearly a foot thick. As the engine was switched off, the creaking of the carts broke the quiet. A small temple was by the side of the airport building, and the evening sun shone on the figure of a scarlet elephant just inside the temple itself. The priest, naked from the waist up, chest touched by a long, straggly beard, stood watching as the Mannerings and Ramdhal walked stiffly towards the building.

A small carriage with big wheels moved slowly along the road, drawn by an old nag and driven by a hopeful-looking old man who waved his whip.

"We will take the tonga," Ramdhal said. "It is a mile to the palace, sahib. I shall be next to the driver." He put their two suitcases on the back of the little carriage, and the driver beamed at them and maintained a constant chatter which neither of them understood. A seat just large enough for two faced the road behind the driver. The road was metalled and thick with dust at the sides; the oxen kicked up clouds of dust with every heavy step. Bearded sleepy-looking drivers sat on the carts, watching the Mannerings incuriously. Two dogs came loping along the road, stopped by the temple and then approached the tonga as it jogged along. The seat had once been upholstered, but all the stuffing was out of it. The vehicle clattered noisily on its iron-bound wheels.

"Real India," Mannering said.

"Mother India," said Lorna. She didn't smile. "I hope you haven't done the wrong thing."

"Feeling isolated?"

"Aren't you?"

A car was coming along the road towards them, turning a corner as Mannering spoke. Its nearside wheels were in the dust and a great cloud billowed behind it. It shone with polish, and there was a youthful Indian driver at the wheel. He made his horn blare as he passed an ox-cart, and the driver hastily pulled into the side of the road. The car came on, then pulled up almost level with the tonga, tyres squealing. The driver jumped out.

"From His Highness," said Ramdhal in a whisper.

"You are Mr. Mannering?" The driver was standing beside the tonga, which had stopped. His Highness the Maharajah told me to put this car at your disposal; please to use it. Your luggage, also." He switched into his own language and appeared to be hurling insults at the driver of the tonga. Ramdhal jumped down and helped Lorna, then Mannering. He paid the driver, and obviously satisfied the man.

The car driver seemed determined to force everything off the road. Lorna clutched Mannering's arm as they swerved past the ox-waggons and a train of donkeys which carried enormous loads.

"Prefer the tonga?" Mannering asked.

"I wouldn't like to go far in this."

Soon the car swung between massive iron gates and they passed from the dusty road, with dry, parched land on either side, into rolling parkland. The transition was abrupt, hardly real. The grass on either side was bright green. Palms, trees they didn't recognise, a few pine and many flowering bushes gave gentleness and beauty. The slanting rays of the sun reddened the tops of the bushes.

They passed beneath an archway cut in a thick hedge of cypress, and the palace stood in front of them; beyond rose and flower gardens which had an almost hurtful beauty of colour. The palace itself, stark white, stretched for what seemed an illimitable distance on either side.

Gardeners were working among the flower-beds; water hissed gently from half a dozen hoses.

The car pulled up in front of the main entrance. Three men stood there, two servants dressed in white, and one white man. The white man raised a hand in greeting.

"Hi, John Mannering!"

"Why, hullo," said Mannering, as he climbed out. "Long way from New York." He helped Lorna out. "Darling, this is Mark Petter. Competition!" He shook hands with Petter, one of the biggest dealers in New York. "How are you, Mark?"

"I'm just fine."

"Looking after you well?" Mannering glanced at the servants who were moving off with his luggage.

"Like a prince."

"And the others?"

"Kyneton's resting. He doesn't like the heat." Kyneton was another New York dealer. "Duval is in bed, sick. The poor fellow ate something that didn't agree with him; he may be in bed for a few days. Van Groot is with His Highness, looking at some pictures."

"Is Duval really in a bad way?"

"I guess he could be worse." Petter strolled up the wide white steps; they looked like marble. "He's feeling mighty sorry for himself, and afraid he'll miss the party." Petter's drawl was attractive. He was nearly as tall as Mannering, blond, forty-odd, with wide shoulders and an easy carriage. He wasn't handsome, but his round face and blue eyes gave him a wholesome look. "You weren't expected so early. When they saw the plane, they did some guessing; that's how I knew it was you."

"I thought I'd see what the hospitality was like for unexpected guests."

"Are you kidding?" Petter said lazily. "If ever you do the expected, I guess Mrs. Mannering will fall down in a faint. Isn't that so, Mrs.

Mannering?"

"You obviously know him," Lorna said.

"Oh, only by reputation and an occasional meeting in London. When are you coming to New York, John?"

"One of these fine days."

They had walked through a long, narrow passage, with photographs of groups of people and racing pictures on either side. They came to a doorway, and Lorna stopped and raised her hands involuntarily. Petter's lips twitched with amusement. Mannering glanced towards the room, and saw a vast chamber, with huge mirrors all round, and chandeliers hanging from the ceiling, so big that they seemed fantastic. Each had hundreds of electric lamps. The furniture was light and delicate, all painted gilt; it was a golden room.

"Not bad," said Petter. "Wait until you've seen the rest, Mrs. Mannering. Before I came here they told me that things were being evened out in India. Now I've seen this and had a look at the village outside, I guess I'm not so sure about that."

A man came out of another doorway, dressed in white drill, youngish, dark-skinned. He bowed distantly to the trio and went into the grounds.

Mannering felt a sharp quickening of suspicion, for he had seen that man before. He had been at Patel's house, one of two men who had sat so quietly for a while – and one of two men who had given chase to a thief and had thrown knives.

"That's Rudra," Petter said in his lazy voice. "His Highness's secretary. Unless I miss my guess, His Highness is on the way here right now."

CHAPTER TWENTY-THREE

THE MAHARAJAH OF GANPORE

As Petter spoke, two men came round a corner of the passage. The first was tall, slim, honey-coloured, with greying dark hair which alone gave him an air of distinction. Mannering judged him to be in the sixties. He had fine, dark eyes, and his features were perfect. Jagat was like him, but not so good-looking. He was dressed in a light-grey suit of faultless cut. He came forward with hand outstretched.

"It *is* Mr. Mannering?"

"Yes."

"I am very pleased you are here. And Mrs. Mannering." He took Lorna's hand and bowed. "I had been told that you would not arrive until tomorrow. We have been waiting for you, and all the others have been very patient. I—but forgive me. Mynheer van Groot – Mrs. Mannering, Mr. Mannering."

The second man was short and stocky, with heavy features, heavy-lidded eyes. Mannering knew him by sight, but had never met him before. His name was famous. His headquarters were in Amsterdam, but his market was the world.

"I am glad to meet you." His voice was harsh. He jerked his head to Lorna.

"How are you?" Lorna said.

"I've been looking forward to seeing you," said Mannering.

"You are both tired from the journey," said the Maharajah. He was as pleasant and unassuming as if he had been one of the guests, and his English was perfect. "I will have you taken to your rooms. We will meet for sherry."

He led the way up a wide flight of stairs. Although he hadn't spoken, hadn't appeared to do anything, two servants appeared and followed silently. Ramdahl was just behind them. They reached the first floor, and the Maharajah led the way along wide passages, with oil paintings hanging on the walls and here and there a tapestry worth a fortune. Everything Mannering saw would have brought dealers from all over the world to Quinns.

They stopped by a pair of double doors.

"Do take your time, Mrs. Mannering. I shall look forward to seeing you when you are ready."

He smiled, and, as the servants opened the doors, turned back to the stairs.

There were three rooms all furnished with the elegance of the Regency days, and a bathroom the size of a small house. The sunken bath was pale green; the walls were of the same colour; the ceiling, too. There were thick mats round the sides of the bath, and two showers in small cubicles.

Ramdahl was waiting in one of the outer rooms.

"Is it all clear?" asked Mannering. "I want you to find out what precautions are taken against theft and, if possible, to find out where the jewels are kept. And make sure whether anyone takes any special interest in me."

"Very good, sahib."

The Mannerings stood together in the doorway of the bathroom.

"Everything a man could want after a long journey," Mannering said. "What do you think of the Maharajah?"

"No robes," said Lorna faintly.

"No penetrating eyes."

"No cortège of bearers."

"No ceremony," said Mannering.

"I suppose he's real?"

"Even human. Bath, ma'am?"

"Do you think I dare soak for half an hour?"

"You won't miss anything but sherry and chatter," Mannering

said. "What did you think of van Groot?"

"Hostile?" asked Lorna. "Unfriendly? Suspicious?"

"Could be all three. He's known to be greedy, and he probably has more millionaires up his sleeve than anyone else in our wicked game. Petter?"

"I liked him."

"Just his American charm," said Mannering. "When it comes to business he'll be as ruthless as the crocodiles in the lakes of Bombay." He was taking off his clothes and moved across to one of the showers, in singlet and trunks. Ramdhal was unpacking the cases in the other room. "Four of the biggest diamond and jewel merchants in the world under one spacious Indian roof, a smooth and suave host with a curious history plus a record of social reform. Notice much social reform outside?"

"No."

"Plus a man named Rudra whom I saw at Patel's house and is the great man's secretary."

"You're dreaming!"

"I'm not likely to forget that face. Plus a gang known as the Bundi, possibly fanatical zealots, possibly just crooks, certainly murderous. Plus what?"

"A sleepy American we haven't seen – what was his name?"

"Kyneton. Pronounced, as you heard, Kine-ton. The most wide-awake American I've met. I don't know him well. I do know that he comes from the south, and I can't imagine why the heat has got him down like this unless it's a normal daily siesta. Plus?"

"Darling," said Lorna, and Mannering stepped out of his trunks and into the shower, "are you trying to scare me?"

"What on earth makes you think that?"

"I'm not appreciating it. Plus what, were you going to say?"

"Guess."

"A sick Frenchman."

"That's right. Four of the biggest men in the jewel business here in Ganpore, pretty well cut off from any civilisation, the Bundi threatening, and two of the dealers already under the weather."

"Five," said Lorna.

"Don't start getting hallucinations." Mannering was vigorous with the soap, but brief.

"Five of the biggest men in the jewel business."

Mannering turned off the water and took the towel which Lorna thrust forward.

"Thanks. Sweetheart, you flatter me. That's all right provided you don't really think it. Compared with any one of these men, I'm small fry. They have more customers who can sign a cheque for millions than I have who can sign cheques for a hundred thousand."

He unzipped the back of her dress and let it slip from her shoulders. He covered his eyes with his hands.

"Darling," said Lorna. "You've some silly idea in your head which probably won't stand up to any kind of examination. What is it?"

She wore a brassiere and the briefest panties.

"You're wonderful!" Mannering grinned.

All outward show of lightheartedness had gone when he went downstairs. The servant outside the door of their suite didn't surprise Mannering; nor did the servants at every door. The servants were all immaculate in white, and the buttons on their tunics were brass, or gold. They were small, dark, lithe-looking men from the hills.

Lights were on – small chandeliers in the wide passages. Only corner lights shone in the big room. Voices sounded from another, not far away. This was much smaller, and furnished almost in modern style; almost, because there were touches which one would only find in the east – the rich cushions and the tapestries and an atmosphere it was hard to define.

Petter and a short, round, tubby man were there – Kyneton. He heard Mannering come in, and pirouetted round, agile as a ballet dancer. He beamed at Mannering as he stretched out his hand.

"Why, hullo there. Just the man I'm glad to see; you can explain everything." He had a softer voice than Petter's. Twenty-five years of New York hadn't changed him, he was still a man from the deep south. His hand grip was firm. "How are you doing, John?"

"Fine, Frank, thanks."

"You look it."

"Not more than ten years older," Mannering said. "Do the doors close?" There were two of the small dark men at the doorway.

"Haven't dared try," said Petter.

"Could go up to our room," said Kyneton. "We share."

"Too obvious," said Mannering. "Obvious that we were going into a huddle, I mean." He kept his voice low, they were in a corner of the room, it wasn't likely that what he said could be heard from the doorway. "That's if you two want to."

Petter slid both hands into his pockets. His suit couldn't have come from anywhere but New York or Washington.

"I remember," he said. "You're a detective, aren't you? That makes you mysterious. We don't mind, do we, Frank?"

Kyneton said: "I guess not."

"All right," said Mannering. "You're after the Maharajah's jewels – so are the others. You're here with your eyes open. You know about Phiroshah's two sons, about the robbery in London. You know there's a hot campaign to steal jewels from the Indian princes under the cover of a patriotic organisation."

"Sure we know," Petter agreed.

"And we know that Phiroshah brought you because of your detective instinct." Kyneton was mildly sardonic. "He doesn't think the police are doing all they could. Do you?"

"I'd like to know why we're all here together."

"He wants to sell his stuff to the highest bidders," said Kyneton. "He knows there's a big risk sending it out of India to sell it. So he'll sell it here, and we'll have to take it out. The Bundi will go for him but not for us."

"Why not?"

"International complications."

"That didn't stop the London robbery or a murder in New York."

Petter said: "I guess not."

Kyneton spoke uneasily: "What's on your mind, John?"

"That we're to be taken for a ride," said Mannering. "Whether by His Highness or not—" He broke off. A shadow appeared on the floor of the passage and stopped moving. "And I think we're going to see the most fabulous collection of jewels we've ever come across," Mannering added mildly.

The shadow moved, and the Maharajah appeared.

"I hope I shall not disappoint you," he said.

He could have heard much more than the last sentence.

CHAPTER TWENTY-FOUR

THE FIFTY-ONE JEWELS

THE Maharajah was smiling. There was nothing to indicate that he had heard more than Mannering's last few words, but he had made sure that they knew he had heard that. Except for his honey-coloured skin, he looked European – more European than swarthy van Groot, who came in just after him. Duval followed. Duval was tall, thin, elderly – French enough to maintain a small beard and waxed moustaches. Mannering thought that he looked ill. He drooped. There was no vitality in his voice when he spoke, or in his grip when he shook hands.

Rudra came a few minutes afterwards, when a servant was handing round sherry – a superb Spanish sherry.

"Is Mrs. Mannering too tired to come down?" asked the Maharajah.

"No, Highness." Mannering used the title deliberately. "She wouldn't miss this for the world!"

"I'm very glad. I'm only sorry that she will be the only woman. I was hoping that my son would bring Shani, but I understand that it will not be possible. And he has been delayed – he thought that you were coming tomorrow."

"I changed my mind," said Mannering, poker-faced.

"To our advantage. By the way, Mannering, we have no ceremony here. No titles, please. You are Mannering, I am Kalda. You see, I am more western than oriental!" His smile flashed. "After dinner we will see the jewels, and you will all have an opportunity of assessing them. Tomorrow, we will get to the business of buying and selling—I hope. More sherry, Petter?"

"Sure. Thanks."

Kalda waved to a servant.

They were talking and laughing, when Lorna came in.

She had packed a black evening gown, without Mannering knowing. It was high at the neck, but her arms and her lovely shoulders were bare. She wore black net gloves up to her elbows, and her hair was piled up in a fashion she seldom adopted, except for occasions where she really wanted to cause a sensation. Watching the faces of the men, she smiled serenely. She had made her sensation; she made them forget everything for the next half-hour, even the fifty-one blue diamonds. Van Groot changed from being gruff and surly; his eyes positively glowed. Even Duval perked up.

Now and again Mannering caught her eye. She was thoroughly enjoying herself.

Dinner was served in a small room, lighted with candles. A long narrow table, highly polished, with mats of exquisite lace; wine of a quality that was almost forgotten in Europe; a host of the silent, dark-skinned servants, trained to perfection; food which brought a glow to Duval's eyes and made him forget his indisposition.

It was nearly eleven o'clock when they had finished.

"The jewels will be displayed in here," said the Maharajah. "I suggest that we all come back in a little more than half an hour."

"Now you know why I brought you along," said Mannering, when they were back in their suite. "You're to distract their attention. They won't think about jewels while you're in the room."

"It seemed the right occasion," said Lorna. "I wore a sari to get out of the Taj Mahal."

"I've forgiven you."

"Thank you, dear. Anything new?"

"The other dealers think the Bundi will go for the Maharajah but not for us or them. We can buy the stones and take them away. Surface reasoning, which wouldn't convince them if they weren't after a collection of jewels that's probably never been equalled and will make a fortune for them. I think Duval and van Groot are nervous, Kyneton less confident than he pretends. Petter's always ready to take risks."

"Ah," said Lorna. "Do you still think you'll find Shani here?"

"I shouldn't be surprised."

"Can you explain Shani's disappearance?"

"Someone wants a weapon to use against old Phiro." There was a sound at the door, and he looked round and saw Petter coming in. The servant on duty outside appeared for a moment, then closed the door.

"I hope I'm not intruding," said Petter.

"I knew you couldn't keep away for long." Mannering offered cigarettes. "How's your blood-pressure?"

Petter glanced at Lorna.

"Quickening."

"Keep it steady for a while," said Mannering. "Have you a ceiling for the blue diamonds?"

Petter thrust his hands in his pockets and looked absurdly boyish.

"No. Frank and I are going to buy them between us, whatever the price."

"Absolutely no ceiling?"

"None."

"Let me buy them," said Mannering.

Lorna stood up.

"John—"

"You heard me, John," said Petter quietly.

"Oh, on a gentleman's agreement. I bid higher than anyone else, but with your money. You take them over as soon as I have them, at the same price. No commission, no tricks."

Petter considered.

"I guess Frank would come in on that. Sure, go ahead. What's the idea?"

"I don't want to let them out of my sight—for long," Mannering said.

"I wish I could be sure that India hasn't turned your head," Lorna said tartly.

"No more than it's always been turned." Mannering glanced at his watch. "Fifteen minutes to go. Shall we have a stroll in the grounds?"

"Watch out for mosquitoes," Petter said. "You'll find a little bottle of stuff in your bathroom cabinet – put a spot or two of that on, it'll keep the little pests away."

Others were also taking the air. The Dutchman and the Frenchman were on the drive, Kyneton at the top of the steps. Petter stayed with him, and Mannering heard them talking in low-pitched voices. Mannering and Lorna strolled across the grass, watching the stars over the distant hills. The palace was on sloping ground, and they could see the lights of the city of Ganpore. Lights from the palace shed a glow over the grounds.

Duval and van Groot were the first to go in. The Americans followed, Mannering and Lorna stayed until the last minute.

The doors of the room where they had had dinner were closed. They stood in a little group outside it, and no one had anything to say. Van Groot was trying unsuccessfully to be phlegmatic. The Frenchman fidgeted, walked up and down, couldn't take his gaze away from the door. Mannering smoked. Lorna stared into the grounds.

There was a sound at the doors, they opened, and the Maharajah stood with a hand on each. He was dressed as he had been at dinner, except for a green turban with a single diamond in it. He smiled gently. Something of the excitement that touched the others also touched him. He bowed, before he stood aside. Duval went forward, hesitated, stood stiffly while Lorna went in. None of the men looked at her.

A single light, hung from the ceiling, specially made to throw its white glow on to the table beneath – a round table.

It was a table of fire.

Sight of it brought Lorna to a standstill, made each of the men stop. Duval actually cried out. Van Groot put a hand to his head, as if it had started to ache. Kyneton gripped Petter's arm. Mannering, behind them all, was the last to see the table in all its glory.

The fifty-one blue diamonds, taken out of their settings, were arranged in a centre-piece fashioned like a cone and covered with black velvet. They were spaced at intervals of about an inch, in two rows which ran right round the cone. One was placed on top, flat; the others set into the velvet.

It seemed like a fiery blue cone, and it held them enthralled.

To Mannering, the most remarkable thing was not the sight of the blue diamonds; nor of these men, all of them used to precious stones, all of them hardened to beauty, standing entranced. It was the effect of the blue diamonds on the other jewels there.

These were arranged on the surface of the table, also on black velvet. They were in clusters. Only occasionally, at great exhibitions or at fabulous private shows, had he seen such a collection. Diamonds, pearls, emeralds, rubies, all there, each with its own beauty and its own sublime brightness. Each cluster would have gladdened the heart and the eye of any collector, and there were ten of them, yet their perfection was dulled by those blue beauties.

It had been done deliberately. Why?

The life and the fire in the centre-piece forced the eyes from the others, showed the blue diamonds in their unique perfection. They scintillated and flamed, could not fail to feed the fire of desire. It was superb showmanship.

The group stood as a tableau for a long time; then Mannering moved and the others followed suit, going right round the table, their attention still riveted on the centrepiece, the other jewels hardly noticed.

Everyone was silent.

Servants stood at each corner, two men together; and there were four at the doors.

The guests came slowly to life. Mannering felt Lorna's hand touch his. Perhaps for the first time she felt the magic in precious stones, felt the heart of the fire which burned in his veins. He damped it down, daren't miss a trick. This was done so that all of them should be blinded by the beauty and filled with gnawing desire; to force the price up. But was that all?

The Maharajah spoke.

"If everyone is ready, we will have a little more light. Then you can examine the stones more closely."

Duval turned away from the table, went to a chair and sat down, weakly. Other lights came on, none of them too brilliant, but detracting from the glory on the table. Van Groot and Kyneton went nearer to the table. Petter looked at Duval. He was pale and trembling.

The Maharajah went across to him.

"Perhaps you would be wise to rest, M. Duval. There will be plenty of opportunity—"

"No, no. I shall recover." Duval dabbed his forehead. The Maharajah motioned to a servant, who brought brandy.

Lorna, close to Mannering, whispered: "Are you expecting anything?"

"Anything," said Mannering.

Van Groot made the first comment.

"It is—more than I expected." The words seemed grudging; in fact, he knew that no words could do this justice. "Eh, Kyneton?"

"Sure. Sure, much more."

"The one gave me the idea," said van Groot. "Just the one. But this—it is almost too much."

"I shall leave you for a few minutes," said the Maharajah in a quiet, casual voice. "You will forgive me." He went towards the door.

He hadn't reached it before the shot came from outside; a single shot at first, sharp and clear; then a volley. The servants stiffened, every man thrust his hand inside his tunic. Lorna leaned against Mannering. The others swung round towards the door. Another outburst of shooting came, much nearer. The doors were open, flashes of flame showed in the grounds.

Men from the passages rushed towards the door as the shooting drew still nearer.

CHAPTER TWENTY-FIVE

HIGH BID

THE room was opposite one of the doors which overlooked the grounds. Mannering moved towards the passage and the little dark-skinned men outside ran into the grounds, firing as they went. Duval moaned. The Maharajah showed for a moment against the side of the door, his hand moved, and darkness dropped on to the room.

Duval moaned again. "The—Bundi."

Mannering turned, heard a sliding sound and peered towards the jewels. He could see nothing. A servant impeded him, he side-stepped, and bumped into Kyneton.

The shooting outside grew fiercer. Now that the room was dark, Mannering could see what was happening in the grounds more clearly. Men darted from bush to bush; the crackle of rifle and revolver fire seemed unending. In the room, Duval was groaning, van Groot was rapidly becoming impatient with him. Petter said: "Are you all right, Mrs. Mannering?"

"Yes."

"Please," said the Maharajah in a sharp voice. 'This way." He was still by the door, and shone a torch towards the ground just behind him.

Mannering was last out.

"Upstairs, to the right," said the Maharajah. "Follow me, please." There was another sliding sound, and this time Mannering saw the doors sliding into position. The shooting outside seemed to have slackened. White-clad figures still darted to and fro. One shot came close to the house, making Duval exclaim again. Van Groot was helping the Frenchman up the stairs.

They went into a small room, of greys and blues. The Maharajah said: "Please help yourselves. I will soon be with you." He went off hurriedly.

Petter moved towards a cocktail bar, which was open; everything anyone could want to drink was there. Duval collapsed into a chair. Kyneton looked a little, round, pugnacious ball of a man.

"Who'll have a highball while the Bundi boys are dealt with?" asked Petter.

"Give me a whisky straight," said Kyneton.

"For M. Duval – brandy," muttered van Groot. "The Bundi. These fanatics have dared—"

"Sure, brandy." Petter was as expert as any barman. He poured out and asked: "Mrs. Mannering?"

"I think I'll have gin and tonic."

"Mannering?"

Mannering was nearest the door.

"Later, thanks," he said. He stepped outside, on Lorna's exclamation of protest. He hurried along the empty passage, opened a door on the left and entered a room which overlooked the grounds and the fight. From its large balcony, the whole scene stretched out in front of him. The shooting was further away, in a corner of the grounds.

There was a rustle of sound behind him.

"Sahib," said Ramdhal, "you should be with the others."

"I wanted a grandstand view." He and Kana's man stood looking out into the night. "What have you discovered?"

"Very little, sahib."

"How far is it from here to the tomb?"

"By road, sahib, nearly a mile and a half."

"As a bird would fly?"

Ramdhal shrugged in the gloom. "Three-quarters of a mile, perhaps, sahib; it is said there is a tunnel."

"Have I been watched?"

"I have seen no one, sahib."

"They might even decide I'm fooled by it all. Ramdhal, during the night you'll see a tall Sikh come out of my room. Don't interfere with him. Warn him if he is seen by anyone else – you can find a way of doing that. Warn him if there appears to be any kind of danger."

"I understand, sahib."

"That's all," said Mannering. "One day I will find a way to thank you."

He saw the flash of a shot some way off, and heard the report. All was quiet in the grounds near the palace. He went back to the others. Lorna's eyes sparkled relief and reproach when she saw him. Duval and van Groot had gone; Petter and Kyneton were near the cocktail cabinet; only Kyneton was drinking.

"Been detecting?" asked Petter.

"Just having a look. The Maharajah seems to have been pretty well prepared. Has he been back?"

"No. Who wouldn't be prepared, with that lot at stake?" said Petter.

Kyneton said: "If the Bundi gang is prepared to fight a pitched battle to get them, how in the hell can we get them out of the place?"

"Strong escort to the airfield, and then flight," said Mannering. "Oh, that wouldn't offer a lot of difficulty." He laughed. "Still in the market?"

"Yes," growled Kyneton.

"Nothing's changed," Petter said. He smoothed down his hair. "I've seen everything now. From the Koh-i-noor in the British crown jewels to this place. I'd never seen anything like those jewels and I guess I never will again. Unless it's the same thing. I haven't recovered yet. Duval couldn't stand it. I can understand the way he felt, too – it was like a physical shock. Don't you agree, Mrs. Mannering?"

Lorna said: "It was the most beautiful collection I've ever seen."

"Goes for us all," Kyneton said jerkily.

The door opened and the Maharajah came in, immaculate and unruffled. He walked across to the cocktail cabinet, glanced round to make sure that all their glasses were filled, and helped himself to a whisky and soda.

"I am sorry about that, but not really surprised. I have feared for some time that there would be attempts to steal the diamonds. You know of the Bundi. I shall be glad when the jewels are off my hands! The precautions which I have taken can only last for a short time, but they are at your disposal, gentlemen. Once out of India, there will be much less danger. You were not too worried, I hope, Mrs. Mannering."

"Just scared out of my wits," said Lorna simply.

"Naturally. I am sorry there was no opportunity for a closer inspection of the other jewels. It will be all right now. M. Duval isn't well enough to return, but Mr. van Groot will be downstairs when we go." He finished his drink. "Mrs. Mannering, what will you have?"

"Nothing, thanks."

Kyneton said: "Kalda, why not get it over with tonight ? Let's bid."

The Maharajah frowned.

"I guess Duval won't be able to take any part, but he wouldn't know what he was doing, anyhow," Kyneton said.

"Let us go below," temporised the Maharajah.

Nothing had really changed.

The doors were closed, and for a while there was only the one light, shining on the blue diamonds; but after a while other lights were put on, and the rest of the jewels had their due attention. Kyneton said again: "Let's bid."

Van Groot drew a deep breath.

"For the blue diamonds, one hundred thousand pounds."

"One fifty," said Kyneton, promptly.

The four dealers sat in armchairs in different parts of the room. Lorna was on the other side, watching. Rudra, the secretary, who had been at Patel's house, was in a corner with a pad and pencil in front of him. The Maharajah kept standing all the time, looking from one man to another. The tension in the atmosphere was as great as when the shooting had started. The hush was brittle; something would break it at any moment. Van Groot sat upright, Kyneton gripped the arms of his chair, Petter was relaxed, Mannering's eyes were closed and he looked half asleep.

He hadn't made a bid.

Van Groot and Kyneton had done most of the bidding, with a casual nod from Petter coming now and again, after van Groot's last figure. They had reached three hundred thousand pounds, and were going up in ten thousands. At first, van Groot had been swift off the mark, now he was hesitating. He looked from Kyneton to Petter, as if trying to read their minds; then he growled: "Three hundred and ten."

"Twenty," Kyneton said.

A long pause; then: "Thirty," said van Groot.

Kyneton hesitated. Petter lit a cigarette and seemed to lose interest. Mannering took a hand out of his pocket and spoke for the first time.

"Four hundred," he said.

It was as if he had dropped a bomb. Petter sat up abruptly, van Groot swivelled round in his chair and glared, Kyneton glowered. Only the Maharajah looked at Mannering with benign approval. Kyneton looked as if he wanted to protest.

"It is too much!" Van Groot's words were almost inaudible. "I give up."

The Maharajah looked hopefully at the Americans. Petter shook his head, Kyneton jumped up and went to a cocktail tray, took a whisky straight and drank half at one gulp.

The Maharajah bowed to Mannering, glanced at Lorna, smiled as if to himself, went to the round table and selected a diamond pendant from one of the other ten groups. He carried it to Lorna and placed it round her neck; it scintillated against the black dress, white fire with a dozen colours stabbing at it.

"With my good wishes, Mrs. Mannering."

Mannering was smiling so broadly that Kyneton looked disgusted and van Groot insulted. They didn't hear what Lorna said. They saw the Maharajah turn to the table and heard him say quietly: "Shall we go on with the others? I am quite prepared to wait until morning, should you wish."

After a pause, Petter said: "Oh, let's finish it."

"As you wish."

"Finish," said van Groot.

"Sure," said Kyneton.

"I'm not in this," Mannering said, and went across and sat on the arm of Lorna's chair.

The tension had gone, the sensation was over. Three business men bid against each other, with the Maharajah conducting the sale smoothly and Rudra making notes swiftly.

The bidding finished at half-past one.

At half-past three Mannering opened the door of his suite, glanced out, saw only Ramdhal, and went into the passage. Ramdahl looked at him without recognition; the man seemed puzzled as he came forward. He saw a Sikh, the man whom Chopra had created.

Mannering took him into his confidence. "All quiet?"

"Yes—yes, sahib."

"No more talking," said Mannering. "Are you sure that no one else is about?"

"All is silent."

They walked towards the head of the wide staircase. If Ramdhal saw no one, Mannering certainly wouldn't. He looked about him, and out of the window towards the stars. Then he led the way down to the room where the jewels had been displayed. There were no guards. He tried the door; it was locked. He didn't waste time with a picklock, but felt the wall where he had seen the Maharajah touch it, just before the doors had slid too. He felt a knob beneath the electric switch, pressed, and heard the doors slide back.

He went in, beckoning Ramdhal.

He pressed another knob beneath the inside switch, and the doors closed; he examined the knob, pressed it again, and nothing happened; again, and the door opened.

"Go out and press the one outside," Mannering said.

Ramdhal obeyed, and Mannering closed the doors and pressed the knob for the second time. He waited, but the doors didn't open until he pressed for the third time. Ramdhal came in.

"Wouldn't it open before?"

"No, sahib."

"The second press locks it from the inside," Mannering said. He put on the light. The room was empty; even the table had gone. He went slowly towards the centre, peering at the floor. He had heard a sliding sound here earlier. The carpet was richly coloured, closely patterned. He went down on his knees and ruffled the surface with his fingers, while Ramdhal watched impassively. He kept ruffling the pile until he saw what he was looking for – a piece let into the carpet. It was circular, about the size of the table. He put his fingers beneath it at one spot, and it came up. Ramdhal hurried to help.

They lifted the carpet aside; parquet flooring was beneath, smoothly polished, and cut round into a circle. Mannering sat down, cross-legged, and began to press each piece of the wood. Ramdhal, sitting on the other side, did the same thing; he needed little telling what to do.

It was Ramdhal who pressed the piece which set the circular patch of floor in motion. It began to sink beneath the level of the rest of the floor, slowly and without a sound.

CHAPTER TWENTY-SIX

THE TUNNEL

MANNERING moved forward steadily, stepping on to the centre of the moving floor. Ramdhal asked an unspoken question. Mannering shook his head. His weight made no difference to the speed with which the platform moved. It was an age before his head was on a level with Ramdhal's feet.

"Come soon," he called.

The chamber below was small and bare, there was no furniture.

The moving platform drew level with the floor of the chamber, but didn't stop. There was darkness beneath him. Mannering kept quite still, but shone his pencil torch. Soon he was able to see bare stone walls; the tunnel was cut out of solid rock. A long way above, Ramdhal stared over the top of the hole.

The movement ceased.

Mannering shone the torch round. He was in a larger chamber with rock walls close on three sides, nothing near on the other. The darkness here stretched so far that the light of the torch was lost. Mannering stepped off his perch cautiously, shone the torch on to the parquet platform and pressed the spot which Ramdhal had found.

It began to move upwards.

Mannering waited until it was above the level of his head, then shone the torch towards the ground and walked about. The floor was solid, hard, stony. A steel pillar ran up to the room where the jewels had been displayed, and the moving section of the floor went up and down on that, electrically controlled.

He was utterly alone.

He went twenty yards into the void before the thin beam of light shone on the far wall – and on a door. The door was open. It led to a tunnel which stretched a long way in the darkness. Mannering went back to the pillar and waited; five minutes afterwards, he saw the platform moving through the ceiling immediately above his head. Ramdhal appeared. Mannering gave him a hand off the platform before it reached the floor.

Mannering led the way towards the door and then into the tunnel. Twenty yards along there was a recess. The table on which the jewels had been shown stood in the recess, covered with its black velvet, but the jewels weren't there. Mannering studied the wall, and saw that there was a false surface made to look like solid rock. This was a new kind of strong-room. He shone the torch round and it fell on light switches.

"We should make sure no one else is near," Ramdhal said.

"There won't be, this end," said Mannering. "If there were guards, they would be here by now." He pressed on the switch. A good light showed, revealing the wall, which looked more as if it had been carved out of solid rock. He examined it closely, pressing gently everywhere. He found out where the rock was solid and where the surface was false; the pattern was slightly different.

Ramdhal said: "I would like to go further along, sahib."

"All right. Be careful."

Ramdhal went off into the darkness of the tunnel.

Mannering turned back to the wall. There were some boxes and sacks here – rice, canned food and biscuits. He left them, returned to the wall, and kept pressing. Now and again he thought that something gave, but when he pressed more firmly nothing happened. He worked for ten or fifteen minutes before a piece of rock moved. He pressed all round; nothing happened. He unwound the tool-kit from his waist, selected a screwdriver, fixed the handle and levered against the piece of rock.

It came away on a hinge.

Behind it was the lock of a safe.

The Maharajah might have a trick or two in store for thieves, Mannering knew. He stood to one side and examined the lock. It looked impossible to open without the right tools, but he had the tools. He started working, slowly. He could hear Ramdhal's soft, fading footsteps, but nothing else except the noise of his drill.

After ten minutes he had the lock back.

He stood to one side as he opened the door. Nothing happened; it was just the door of a strong-room.

He stepped inside, looked round for the light switch, touched it, and took his hand away. He used the pencil torch for light. He studied the light switch, and saw two cables leading from it; one might be to an alarm.

The torch-light showed the strong-room to be large – fifteen or twenty feet in each direction. Two safes stood against one wall, big but old-fashioned; he would need half an hour to open each. A smaller safe on a shelf would be much easier.

He wasn't only interested in the safes.

There were wooden crates round the walls – two or three dozen of them, piled on top of each other. One of the crates was open, and inside were brown-paper packets. He went across, picked out a packet, and unfastened it; the ends were sealed with gummed tape and he was careful not to tear it. Inside was a white powder.

He wetted his finger on his tongue, dabbed the finger on the powder, and put it to his tongue again. He hardly needed to make the test.

This was cocaine.

Mannering stood looking at the crates and their foul cargo. Here was the connection between Patel and Ganpore; this explained old Patel's scornful rejection of the idea that he worked for someone else.

Here was illusory delight and years of torment for hundreds of thousands of people.

Mannering went to the smaller safe; in five minutes it was unlocked. There were papers inside, mostly bills and lists of machine parts and water-pipes, all charged to Ganpore. In fact, they were for the cocaine.

They were from Patel's company in Bombay.

Mannering went back to the tunnel. Footsteps were drawing nearer now, but only those of one man. He saw Ramdhal's torch-light shining towards the floor. It was cold and dank; he shivered.

Ramdhal loomed up.

"This way," Mannering said.

He still didn't touch the switch, but led the way; the two torches gave a bright light. He shone his on to the open packet. Ramdhal started when he saw it, hurried forward, and made exactly the same test. He swung round.

"You know, sahib?"

"I know," said Mannering.

"Did you know before?"

"It was half a guess. How long will it take you to get out of Ganpore to somewhere from where you can safely telephone Kana?"

Ramdhal said: "There are tons of it. Tons!"

"Yes. How long?"

Ramdhal licked his lips. "What did you say, sahib?"

"How long will it take you to get to a place from where you can safely telephone Kana?"

Ramdhal hesitated. "I am not sure. A day, at most. I could leave here now and walk to the town. I could get a car; yes, I have sufficient money. I should not be recognised in the town, and in any case I have friends who would help me. I could get to the border of the state by tomorrow afternoon and telephone soon after that. Sahib, even if Kana acts at once, he will first need special authority. It will be three days before police could reach here in strength. Perhaps more."

"We can't spare three days. Two."

"I can ask, sahib."

"Kana will manage it in two," said Mannering. Kana might even come earlier. "But first, tell Kana everything." He was smiling tautly. "What did you find?"

"A door which I could not open – a steel door."

"It probably leads to the tomb," said Mannering, half to himself. "We're facing east; the tomb is due east from the palace. The tomb is sealed, I suppose."

"Always."

"So we can't get you out that way. We'll get back. Take this." Mannering pushed the packet of cocaine into Ramdhal's hand as they moved towards the door. In the tunnel, he spoke softly. "You start, Ramdhal; get out of the palace as soon as you can. Send the lift back for me."

"I shall wait for you."

"You won't. I've a lot of work to do."

Ramdhal said: "I will go."

Mannering stood alone, outside the wall of the strong-room. It was closed and locked. If anyone examined it they would see that it had been forced; there was nothing he could do about that. He pushed the piece of wall which concealed the lock into position, then turned towards the tunnel and the 'lift'. There had been no sound since Ramdhal had gone, nearly half an hour ago.

Mannering had done nothing but close the doors and set the lock again; it could not be opened without keys now; it would need a close inspection to show that it had been forced. He walked towards the platform lift, and the coldness caught at him. He shivered, partly from reaction. He went out of the narrow tunnel into the wider chamber. The platform was waiting. He stepped on to it and pressed the piece of parquet with his foot. It began to rise.

There was no need for alarm, yet alarm was in him. It had all gone so smoothly, too smoothly.

He passed through the first chamber.

His head was on a level with the floor of the room where all of them had gathered a few hours ago. He was facing the door. He watched it tensely as the floor raised him. He was waist high, when he climbed out. He went to the corner of the room, level with the door. Now he watched the circular platform rising; now he watched the door.

He heard voices, footsteps.

He felt his heart thumping. The platform wasn't yet in position. If anyone came in and saw it rising, they would know that he had been below. He found himself gripping his gun tightly, with clammy fingers.

The voices were just outside.

The platform came to a stop.

Mannering moved swiftly, facing the door all the time, bent down and pulled the carpet into position. A piece of it folded under, it seemed an agony of time before he got it straight. He stood up and went to the door, stood just behind it, against the wall.

The voices continued, a muttering in the language of the state. He couldn't understand a word.

Had Ramdhal been caught?

He felt tension increasing, and fought against it. He watched the door, as if it magnetised him, and he saw it sliding back. Of course – Ramdhal had not been able to lock it from the inside.

The door opened wide. One of the dark-skinned men came in; another followed; a third. They went straight to the middle of the room without looking at the door. He stepped slowly towards the passage. If one glanced round, he would be seen. Once the alarm was raised, the safe and the strong-room would be examined, the forced lock would be found.

He reached the passage, stepped to the right, and was out of sight of the men in the room. He walked quickly but without hurrying to the stairs, then ran up them; the carpet muffled the sound. He stopped at the landing. Leaning over the banisters, he could see into the passage, and the door of the showroom.

The men came out, without haste, the door slid to and the men went off – two in one direction, one in the other. None of them approached the stairs.

Mannering stopped at the door of his own room and turned the handle slowly and almost fearfully. Could he get away with it? Would something go wrong now?

He stepped inside.

The outer room was empty.

He locked the door, leaned against it for a moment, and then went across to the cocktail cabinet, poured himself a neat whisky, and tossed it down. He dropped into a chair and sat there for five minutes. At last he crept into the bedroom. Lorna was lying with one arm crooked above her head, peaceful as a child. He went into the bathroom and began to clean off the make-up. Now that he was so near safety, his nerves tore at him savagely.

Mannering went back into the bedroom in his pyjamas. Lorna hadn't moved. He got into bed and switched off the little light which had been on all the time. He lay on his back. It was nearly half-past five, and the household was stirring; he heard sounds inside and outside. He wondered if Ramdhal had got his car. He wondered what would happen in the morning. How Duval was. Whether a trick would be played with the blue diamonds. Neither Kyneton nor Petter had complained about the way he had jumped from three hundred and forty thousand pounds to four hundred thousand. Kyneton would certainly complain bitterly that he could have got them for much less, that van Groot had reached his limit.

He found himself smiling.

He went to sleep.

It seemed that he had been asleep only for a few minutes when he felt himself shaken, heard Lorna's voice, low-pitched but urgent. His eyes were heavy, his head was like lead. He didn't want to wake up, but Lorna's voice grew more and more insistent. He opened his eyes, saw her face close to his, filled with alarm.

"John, you must wake up. You *must* wake up. Ramdhal says he must see you at once."

CHAPTER TWENTY-SEVEN

PRISONERS?

MANNERING pushed back the bedclothes and sat up. Lorna moved away, and Ramdhal stood between the bed and the door, dismay vivid in his face.

"I am sorry, sahib; it is impossible to leave Ganpore. There are roads through the mountain passes, and all of them are blocked. It was my good fortune to fall among friends, who warned me of this. All roads have been blocked for people going out, for several days. The only way is over the mountains themselves, and that will take a long time."

Lorna brought a sponge and towel, sat on the side of Mannering's bed, spread the towel over his knees and handed him the sponge.

"If I'd known you were going to be up half the night I'd have chained you to the bed," she said.

"On Dr. Weiner's advice," murmured Mannering. "Ramdhal, there must be another way out."

"To the north only, sahib. That would also take a long time, and you would be in the mountains again. It is not possible to leave without the Maharajah's authority. No one may go. I have done the only thing I could."

Mannering said: "What?"

"I have arranged with a friend to go across the hills into the next state. It will take him at least three days. He will telephone Kana then. But even if he gets through, it will now be four and perhaps five days before Kana can come."

Mannering said slowly: "At least there's a time limit. Thanks, Ramdhal."

"What is all this?" asked Lorna.

"It doesn't look as if the Maharajah wants us to leave yet. Ramdhal and I found snow by the ton last night. You know, coc—"

"I know snow is cocaine," said Lorna. The colour had gone from her cheeks and yet her eyes were suddenly bright. "Are you sure?"

"Positive. Ramdhal went to take a message to Kana, but couldn't get away. We don't know exactly what he's up to yet, but if he finds out that the strong-room was burgled—"

"*You* found the strong-room?"

"All I took was a broken packet of snow," protested Mannering virtuously. "I gave that to Ramdhal." He sponged his face and dried himself. "What's the time?"

"John," said Lorna, "did you expect to find cocaine?"

"Let's say I hoped to," said Mannering.

Lorna sat down heavily on a chair by the side of the bed.

"Patel was in it," Mannering went on. "Patel's main business has been drugs. Jewels as a sideline, perhaps, but drugs, drugs and more drugs. Kana told us so; we know that Patandi was just one of hundreds of agents who distributed. We also knew that Patel was in this jewel sideline – he and his heirs. So both drugs and jewels were involved. Ganpore is a little state, hidden away from the others, so far off and so insignificant in the eyes of a government which has plenty on its hands, that it was left to run itself almost autonomously. Then there was the Bundi and the war against the jewels belonging to the princes – a war with public opinion on the side of the zealots, making Kana's task ten times more difficult. The Bundi got a lot of jewels, but none has ever been traced on the market. That made Kana and Phiroshah sceptical. Would the Bundi steal just to gloat over the beauty? If the Bundi was a cloak and criminals were behind it, sooner or later they would have to sell. Those diamonds we saw last night aren't all the Maharajah's. They are the proceeds of many thefts from the private collections of different princes, not likely to be recognised by buyers from the West. The blue diamonds are really his. They were to blind us from suspecting the other stolen stuff. Easy enough, isn't it? The Maharajah, the jewel big-shot, worked with Patel, who ran the dope."

Lorna said: "Give me a cigarette, please." They were on the table by Mannering's bed. "So the dealers were brought here to buy stolen jewels that couldn't be smuggled out. And you—"

"I wasn't wanted. Phiro recommended me; the Maharajah didn't write and invite me, but told Phiro he had."

Lorna said: "I see. What—"

She stopped and looked over her shoulder nervously; she need not have done, for Ramdhal was coming in with tea and fruit juice.

"He's as good as Amu," said Mannering lazily.

Ramdhal put the tray down and went out. Lorna lit her cigarette as Mannering poured tea.

"And now we're imprisoned," Lorna said heavily. "I don't understand it. Why? He's sold the jewels. Isn't that what he wanted?"

"He's playing safe. We wouldn't know we were prisoners but for Ramdhal." Mannering finished his tea and pushed back the bed-clothes. "Have you seen any of the others this morning?"

"Van Groot was walking in the grounds."

"Remember that we don't know anything about being hemmed in," said Mannering.

He had a shower and shaved, and was feeling fit enough when he left the suite. Lorna had already gone downstairs. Breakfast was served in the room where they had dined; the long narrow table was now placed over the circular platform. Van Groot sat by himself at one end of the table, Kyneton and Petter were together, eating with obvious appetite. Lorna was opposite the two Americans.

They were sitting and smoking cigarettes when the Maharajah came in briskly.

"Mrs. Mannering, gentlemen. Good morning!" Nothing in his manner suggested that he suspected what had happened. "I hope everyone is well. I have seen poor Duval and my physician is with him now. I am sure you all hope with me that his illness isn't serious."

"Damned bad luck," Petter said.

Van Groot grunted. Kyneton nodded.

"And I hope you are all perfectly happy about our deal," said the Maharajah. "There is the matter of payment, of course, which has to be discussed." He looked at Mannering smilingly. "Yours is the largest account, Mr. Mannering."

"How do you suggest?" Mannering asked.

"You understand, all of you, the difficulties I am in," said the Maharajah. "I can, however, obtain all the credits I need from the Government provided I can show that I have funds abroad. So I am going to suggest that all of you arrange to make payment to my agents in London and New York, by cable, against your cabled request. You can also arrange insurance that way."

No one disagreed.

"It will take two or three days," said the Maharajah.

Van Groot jerked his head up.

"That is not necessary. I am already anxious to go. I have stayed longer than I intended. I am a business man, with much to do. I begin to think I was a fool to come – payment should be against the jewels in Amsterdam or London, not against delivery here. After last night, how can we be sure that we shall get them out?"

"I will see that you have the strongest escort," said the Maharajah smoothly. "I am sorry about the delay. I would gladly accommodate you, but—" He shrugged. "The weather has been bad over central India. Air services have been disrupted, and the plane in which you were to have returned to Bombay, Mynheer, will not be here for at least two or three days."

Van Groot was getting up slowly.

"There is the plane Mannering came in."

"Unfortunately it has developed engine trouble," said the Maharajah. Mannering still couldn't guess whether he knew about the strong-room. "We have wirelessed for the necessary spare parts, but it may be two or three days before they can arrive. I am sorry." He spread out his hands. "I will, of course, hand each of you the jewels you bought. I will provide guards. You will make all arrangements by cable, enjoy yourselves here for a day or two. Duval would not in any case be able to leave; it would be too bad if you were to desert him."

Kyneton sat absolutely still.

Petter said: "Are you saying that you're going to keep us here until the drafts are cleared? What guarantee have we that—"

"My friend, please! It is unavoidable. You need have no worries. The only safe way out is by aeroplane. You saw the attack which was made against us last night. There are dacoits in the hills who would attack you if you attempted to go by road. You will have the jewels and you will be well entertained. Once the weather has improved and the aircraft have arrived—" He shrugged. "Do we need to talk about it any more?"

Van Groot said harshly: "I wish to make myself understood. Not one penny will I pay to your agents. Not one penny – until I have the jewels and am out of Ganpore. I tell you that." He thrust his head forward and glared at the Indian.

Kalda still smiled.

"It is—a mistaken point of view, my friend. You surely understand my difficulty. The dacoits have been a great menace recently. They are not my people. They have come from the famine country beyond the mountains. They can get out of hand. I try, but—"

Petter said quietly: 'This is the coolest frame-up I've ever heard of."

"An ugly expression," murmured the Maharajah.

"It is true!" Van Groot could hardly choke the words out. "It is absolutely true. You would have us murdered—"

"Nonsense," said the Maharajah sharply. "All this fuss, over what? We have reached an agreement; you have bought the jewels. You simply have to pay for them. A few days of delay, because of weather – isn't that the way to look at it?"

"And then you take back the jewels and cut our throats!"

The Maharajah looked distressed.

"Mynheer, I ask you—"

Petter said mildly: "Let's try not to get heated. Where are my stones, Kalda?"

"In my strong-room."

"Good. I'll take delivery now, against my cabled draft to New York."

Mannering felt his heart thump.

"You play into his hands!" cried van Groot.

"Take it easy," Petter said. "If we can't get out, we can't. I don't mind paying for the jewels, provided I have them." His smile was as bland as the Maharajah's. "Once I have them, they're in my custody, no one else's responsibility. If I were you—" he looked at the others smilingly—"I'd take the same course. Delivery of the jewels against the despatch of our cables. After that, we can all keep together, in case the Maharajah should be unable to control the dacoits, but I think he'll manage that for us."

"It's all wrong," Kyneton said. He was pale and his eyes were frightened. "Don't you agree, Mannering?"

Mannering said: "I haven't made up my mind." But he knew the Maharajah would go to the strong-room, and find evidence of burglary.

"Why should we worry?" Petter asked. "We'll have the jewels, he'll have the money. We paid our own price. Nothing wrong about that, was there? Kalda, may I have those diamonds?"

"At once," said the Maharajah.

"Bring my purchase, too," said Mannering.

"It's crazy, but I'd better agree," said Kyneton.

"Van Groot?" the Maharajah asked gently. "It would be better if you were all of one mind."

Van Groot said carefully: "I pay not one penny until I am out of this damn country."

The Maharajah shrugged.

The door closed behind him as he went out.

Van Groot jumped to his feet and hurled a torrent of angry recrimination. Petter went across to Lorna and began to talk. Van Groot dried up, but stood near the door as if prepared to rush out as soon as it opened again.

The jewels were brought into the room on small trays, nearly an hour later. The servants who brought them went out, closing the door. The Maharajah of Ganpore gave no sign of having discovered the evidence of the raid. He motioned to the cases which had been placed on a small table near Mannering.

"Inspect the greatest prize, my friend."

"Thanks." Mannering opened the first case. There were nine small blue diamonds in it; he had seen these diamonds and this case before. In the indifferent light of the room they looked real. He put one of them on the table and peered at it, then slid his hand to his pocket and drew out his automatic. He held it by the barrel, then brought the butt down on to the diamond.

It smashed into a hundred pieces; a fine white powder remained on the table.

The Maharajah backed towards the door, but the gun slid round in Mannering's hand.

"I should stay there, Kalda. Mark, press the knob on the right of the door, twice – it's level with your eyes." Petter obeyed; the door was locked. Mannering looked lazy as he picked up the other nine paste gems in his left hand and tossed them into the air. "That's what they're worth. We don't stand on ceremony here, Kalda, do we? This is the showdown. You took it for granted that after seeing the real diamonds last night we'd give them a cursory glance this morning. And as you were afraid I'd find a way out once I had them, you daren't risk giving me the real stuff."

The Maharajah's eyes were cold with fury. Van Groot was baring his teeth with anger.

"Plain speaking, plain facts. You're a liar, a fraud and a murderer or accomplice of murderers," Mannering went on.

"You worked with or under the protection of the Bundi. Most of the jewels we've bought are stolen. You worked with Patel, who handled the drugs."

No one spoke.

Mannering said: "The big sale might have worked, but these blue jewels have been in your family for so long you didn't want to part with them, but they drew the big dealers here. Oh, the other stuff's genuine. If I'd discovered these fakes after I'd left you'd have said the switch took place after I bought them. Am I going too fast?"

The Maharajah looked his venom.

"You're not going fast enough for me," Petter said.

"What are we going to *do*?" cried van Groot. "We are prisoners; we—" He broke off.

"Remember that," the Maharajah said thinly.

"Remembered." Mannering smiled. "If the worst comes to the worst, Kalda, you can stage another dacoit raid, have us murdered, blame the Bundi. You could probably get yourself a medal trying to defend us."

"*Stage* a raid," Kyneton choked. "Was last night—"

"As phoney as the blue diamonds, arranged to get us into the right frame of mind," Mannering said. "Kalda has used the Bundi, probably a genuine organisation at one time, to cover himself all along. He even sent one blue diamond out of the country, using Phiroshah, to show how anxious he was to sell. I'm guessing, but I think real Bundi agents, misguided zealots, went after those and killed Yusuf Phiroshah in New York. They probably carried out the London robbery, too, and made Phiroshah a tool in Kalda's hands, ready to lend his name to the invitations to the big dealers. But old Phiro named me. Kalda didn't like the idea of an amateur detective around and forgot to invite me. Phiroshah, not knowing that, made sure I came. As the sample diamond was still in Phiroshah's possession, he used that to lure me to India.

"Kalda tried to keep me away – by threats, by a show of force at my shop. He tried to send me back, using kid-glove methods at first. When I stayed, he turned desperate, but he wasn't sure why I stayed, what Phiroshah and I knew. His son was in love with Phiroshah's daughter, might have some idea of the truth, might have told Shani, who would have told her father. He had Phiroshah and I kidnapped, but we got away before his men could question us and find out what we knew. Then he took Shani and his own son – would a man be party to kidnapping his own son? Holding Shani, he felt safe from Phiroshah. Old Patel was dead. He could use his house, have his own son freed – as it happened, I freed Jagat before it was intended – who would pass the message on to me. He, the Maharajah, doubted Phiroshah's honesty. A nice touch. And Jagat had to get me here quickly. Kalda had to know when I started; would have had my plane brought down somehow. So I came ahead of time."

Mannering stopped. No one spoke for what seemed a long time.

Then the Maharajah moved his position slightly, and a taut smile curved his lips.

"You are so clever and talk so much. Tell me, how are you going to take this story to the police?"

"Ah!" ejaculated van Groot. "Is there a way, Mannering?"

CHAPTER TWENTY-EIGHT

THE WAY OUT

THE Maharajah's smile broadened as Mannering stood silent, covering him with the gun. Van Groot repeated harshly: "Is there a way?" No one else spoke.

Mannering said mildly: "Oh yes. After the jewels were shown last night, I had that look round. I made an interesting discovery. By moving the table and pulling up part of the carpet we can get below the palace to the strong-room and the tunnel. That's where we're going. The air's quite fresh down there. There are some iron rations and plenty of rice – I saw that last night, too. We'll take some water, and be able to stay there for a few days."

"It will not help you." But Kalda's smile had lost its edge of triumph.

"Oh, I don't know," said Mannering. "You'll be with us. If any of your people try to get at us, we will simply tell them you'll be killed if there's any trouble. They won't take the chance, will they?"

"How will it help if we lock ourselves up?" demanded van Groot.

"We shan't have to stay long," said Mannering. "I sent a message out last night. It will soon reach the Bombay police, and when they hear about the drugs they will stir up a lively Government interest in Ganpore. Three or four days down there won't be pleasant but won't be unbearable. Will it, Lorna?"

Lorna said chokily: "We'll manage."

"You are lying," said the Maharajah. "No one went out with a message."

"Oh yes. Over the hills. The passes through the mountains were blocked, but there are tracks which a man on a donkey can use." He turned to the others. "I'd have tried to stall without letting Kalda know what I knew if it hadn't been for the blocked passes. He'd get word from there as soon as the police arrived in force, and have time to get rid of us. So he's better staying with us than outside, able to give orders for our quick despatch by dacoits, and able to get rid of the cocaine. We'll wait. The police will come in good time, and – there's the way out! Satisfied, van Groot?"

The Dutchman began to smile.

"Very good," he said. "*Very* good. Now I know that what I hear about you is true. I did not like it when you arrived. Always, they say, you bring trouble. I like your kind of trouble. It is a good way out. I will wait."

"You'll have to," Petter said dryly. "How do we get below, John?"

"Shift the table first," said Mannering. "I—"

He broke off. There were sounds outside, but the door didn"T open. A man called out softly, then more loudly, in the language of Ganpore. The Maharajah took a step forward.

"Talk to him through the door," Mannering said.

"It is Rudra Patel."

"Fine," said Mannering. "Tell him to talk in English."

The Maharajah said thinly: "Mannering, you will not succeed, and when I have turned the tables—"

Mannering called: "Rudra, can you hear me?"

After a moment, Patel's son called back: "Yes, yes, but I must talk to His Highness."

"Through the door, and in English."

"This is private, personal."

"So is the gun in the Maharajah's back," said Mannering.

"Gun!"

"In his back."

The Maharajah said steadily: "What is it, Rudra?"

"Highness—" The man outside seemed to choke. "We—must hurry. There is an aeroplane full of police arriving at the airport. From Bombay. I have just had a telephone call telling me that it left yesterday, with—with Prince Jagat also on board."

Mannering was surprised at the extent of his own relief.

"I'll say we must hurry," said Petter. "The police can't get here soon enough for us. John, did you fix this?"

"It's just a little of my everyday luck," Mannering said.

Kana had come himself, with a high Government official, and all the men required to enforce the law in Ganpore.

Jagat was with them. Rudra's information had been accurate. Jagat, looking pale and haggard and much older than his years, was present when his father was formally arrested. Kalda neither looked nor spoke to his son. Three senior policemen took the Maharajah out of the palace, where he would be taken straight to the aerodrome. Jagat went up the stairs to the window and looked along the drive as his father was driven off in his own car.

Mannering and old Kana went slowly up the stairs after him. The detective, dressed in his western clothes, was frowning as if troubled. Downstairs, the Americans and van Groot were talking excitedly.

Lorna followed the other two up the stairs.

The car disappeared.

Jagat turned away, and there were tears in his eyes. He fought them back, looked at Kana, raised his hands and said huskily: "So I have betrayed him."

"It was right, my son," said Kana gently. "It was right. Your good friend Mannering was here and able to stop what might have been a great slaughter. Had that happened and the truth came out, the name of Kalda and Ganpore would stink in the nostrils of man. You have a chance to work for the state. In the aircraft you told me that was what you wanted. Has it stopped being true?"

Jagat said: "No. No, it is true."

"Of course," said Kana. "Also, you make a poor liar, my son. Isn't that so, Mannering?"

Mannering asked: "What happened to you, Jagat? Why were you kidnapped? What message were you to bring for me?"

"But I tried to tell you." The youth spoke as he looked towards the window again. "On my father's orders, I was to tell you that we did not trust Phiroshah. I did trust him. I am in love with Shani. I know both Shani and her father well; I have no doubt of their honesty.

"I suspected what was being planned, and I had seen cocaine in my father's strong-room.

"I could not bring myself to tell you what I thought, but gave you some clues. I told you what my father instructed, but tried to warn you not to obey. You understood that?" He was suddenly eager.

Mannering smiled.

"You did it well; we'll always be grateful. The kidnapping—"

"Of Jagat, because Shani could not be taken alone," said the detective quietly. "Of Shani—I am not sure, but I think I can guess."

Jagat said: "It was because of Shani that I came to you, Mr. Kana. Shani was kidnapped because my father began to fear Phiroshah might begin to suspect the truth. I had to help her. And there was more. If you saw, as I have seen, the harm done by drugs here in India. If you knew the misery that they inflict, the way in which it worsens a situation already so bad that few of us can see how to improve it—"

Jagat broke off.

"All is well, my son," said Kana. He smiled at Mannering, turned to Lorna, although until then he hadn't shown that he knew she was present. "Shani is safe. We found her in the caves at the lakes. All members of the Patel family have been arrested. There is one other thing that will interest you, Mannering." He gripped Mannering's arm. "Phiroshah will recover. He is a most remarkable young old man!"

Three weeks later, Lorna sat on a couch in a room at the Taj Mahal Hotel, with a sketch pad on her knees and her pencil idle in her fingers. Mannering looked as if he were dozing, in a long chair. He opened his eyes, and Lorna said: "Like a drink?"

"Obstinate woman. Yes, please. Just shout 'Amu' and he'll know what you want at this time of the afternoon."

Lorna called: "Amu!"

The door opened, and Amu asked promptly: "Tea for the

memsahib?"

"Please, Amu."

"At once." Amu withdrew, closing the door quietly.

Mannering laughed.

"Seen enough?" he asked.

"Not nearly enough," said Lorna. "I can close my eyes and see the Taj Mahal and the red forts and the mosques and the beauty and the ugliness, the history and the mystery. It hurts too much when they're close together. I don't want to stay any longer, but I'm glad we came."

"And tomorrow we leave," said Mannering.

"Are you satisfied?"

Mannering said: "I feel rather like you do. At least Phiroshah has taken a new lease of life; Shani's happy; Jagat isn't letting things get him down too much, I'm told. I turned in that necklace I took from Patel's house – an anonymous present to the police – so my conscience is clear. By the way, a wedding present will soon be due. Mind if I make a suggestion?"

"You don't often hesitate."

"I don't often make this kind. Paint Shani for them."

Lorna's eyes kindled.

"Done!" said Mannering. He saw the door open and went on: "Ah, here's tea."

"It wasn't tea, but Phiroshah. He bowed at the door and then came forward slowly, smiling, looking more ancient than ever but with the light of peace in his eyes. He shook hands, and Mannering pushed up a pouf for him.

"Thank you, my friend. I came myself, because I was so pleased at what I have just heard. From Jagat." His eyes were shining. "My daughter is indeed fortunate, and I can say that I have a true son."

The others waited.

"Yes," said Phiroshah, "Jagat will be worthy, whatever he does. He sends the news I have for you. He is to sell all the jewels he inherits and use the money for social work in Ganpore. He will turn the palace into living quarters for hundreds of families, and he and Shani will live in a small house nearby. But that isn't what he asks me to tell you. He would like you to dispose of the jewels. You will, I'm sure."

Mannering murmured: "Why not you?"

"Oh, my friend, I am too old to worry any more about business," said Phiroshah gently. "I told you, I shall sell out soon. You will accept?"

"Gladly. And – thanks."

"Listen to him," said Phiroshah. "He is thanking me. What nonsense he can talk!" He smiled at Lorna, then looked back at Mannering, beginning to frown. "There is one thing which may have puzzled you, Mannering. It did me, for a while. The murder of my sons. The true Bundi killed Yusuf in New York. Misguided zealots, who could blame them? Also they stole those jewels in England, tried to rob you of the blue diamond. But—Ali—Ali, my beloved son. I have the truth of that, now. He was not attacked by dacoits on the way to the Maharajah. He reached the palace safely – and saw enough there to guess what was being planned. He was attacked when leaving the palace, not going to it – and not by dacoits. Did you see the truth about Ali, Mannering?"

"It started me doubting the Maharajah of Ganpore," Mannering said quietly. "Would thieves leave a dying man with a diamond?"

"You see, I am getting old," said Phiroshah. He glanced at the door, as Amu came in with the tea. "Ah! And here is a drink fit for an old one."

The old Hindu smiled at Lorna, as he would at Shani and his sons.

JOHN CREASEY

GIDEON'S DAY

Gideon's day is a busy one. He balances family commitments with solving a series of seemingly unrelated crimes from which a plot nonetheless evolves and a mystery is solved.

One of the most senior officers within Scotland Yard, George Gideon's crime solving abilities are in the finest traditions of London's world famous police headquarters. His analytical brain and sense of fairness is respected by colleagues and villains alike.

'The finest of all Scotland Yard series' – New York Times.

GIDEON'S FIRE

Commander George Gideon of Scotland Yard has to deal successively with news of a mass murderer, a depraved maniac, and the deaths of a family in an arson attack on an old building south of the river. This leaves little time for the crisis developing at home ....

'Gideon of Scotland Yard emerges as one of the most real working detectives in modern fiction.... A sympathetic and believable professional policeman.' - New York Times

JOHN CREASEY

THE CREEPERS

"The prisoner's hand was thin and bony ... And in the centre of the palm was a pinkish mark. It was the shape of a wolf's head, mouth open, fangs showing. Although it was what he had expected to see, Inspector West felt a twinge of repugnance a stab not unrelated to fear. It was the fifth time he had seen the mark of the wolf – the mark of Lobo."

A gang of cat burglars led by Lobo cause mayhem as they terrorize the city. They must be stopped, but with little in the way of evidence the police are baffled. Just how can Inspector West manage to do this in what is a race against time before more victims succumb?

"Here is an excellent novel of law enforcement officers, harried, discouraged and desperately fatigued, moving inexorably ahead under the pressure of knowledge that they must succeed to save human lives." - Cleveland Plain-Dealer

"Furiously exciting" - Chicago Tribune

"The action is fast, continuous and exciting" - San Francisco News

JOHN CREASEY

THE HOUSE OF THE BEARS

Standing alone in the bleak Yorkshire Moors is Sir Rufus Marne's 'House of the Bears'. Dr. Palfrey is asked to journey there to examine an invalid - who has now disappeared. Moreover, Marne's daughter lies terribly injured after a fall from the minstrel's gallery which Dr. Palfrey discovers was no accident. He sets out to investigate and the results surprise even him . . . .

"'Palfrey' and his boys deserve to take their places among the immortals." - Western Mail

INTRODUCING THE TOFF

Whilst returning home from a cricket match at his father's country home, the Honourable Richard Rollison - alias The Toff - comes across an accident which proves to be a mystery. As he delves deeper into the matter with his usual perseverance and thoroughness , murder and suspense form the backdrop to a fast moving and exciting adventure.

'The Toff has been promoted to a place of honour among amateur detectives.' – The Times Literary Supplement

7106086R00108

Printed in Great Britain
by Amazon.co.uk, Ltd.,
Marston Gate.